TERA LYNN CHILDS

Trying Texas

For the yellow coat, and also Erika

ONE

I MUST HAVE DONE something terrible in a past life to deserve this kind of punishment. Really terrible. Like clubbed baby seals and knocked down old ladies in the street terrible.

As I stared out the front window at the long, never-ending stretch of highway, I had to fight the overwhelming urge to fling myself out of the moving SUV. The gray strip of blacktop seemed to go on into infinity. Pure, unabashed nothingness. Isolation surrounded by dust, cows, and—

"Was that a tumbleweed?" I demanded.

Eddie stared straight ahead, eyes on the road like a hypnotized zombie. "Uh-huh."

Had we really been in New York just this morning? It didn't seem possible. My six a.m. caffeine injection and everything bagel with shmear from the deli around the corner from my apartment felt like a lifetime ago. Twelve lifetimes.

As a native Manhattanite, Los Angeles was normally as uncivilized as I was willing to get—and that was only for the few short years of film school because my undergrad advisor thought I should "broaden my experience base" before entering the industry.

But even though New York was half-a-continent closer at the moment than when I had been in California, I'd never felt farther away. I had no idea how much nothingness actually filled the country between the two coasts. I'd never been one of those snotty New Yorkers who considered everything between us and L.A. to be nothing more than a flyover state, but I was starting to think maybe they were right.

Did people actually live here?

Dallas hadn't scared me. It was a big city, after all, with shopping and culture and every amenity a die-hard city girl could want. There had been skyscrapers and traffic noise. Grit, pollution, and panderers at busy intersections. A drugstore with ample supply of my more-necessary-than-ever heartburn medicine.

Sure, the attendant at the car rental desk had a thick accent and said *y'all* a lot—a *lot*—but that was almost charming. I'd actually thought to myself, *Maybe Texas won't be so bad after all*.

But this? This was a different world—a different universe.

A couple hundred miles west from one of the busiest airports in the world in one of the largest metro areas in the country, and I might as well have been on the moon.

Was this even the same planet?

"How long since you had signal?" Eddie asked.

I glanced down at my phone, clutched desperately in my fist.

"Half an hour," I replied. "At least."

Since leaving Fort Worth city limits I'd seen more cows than cars and more abandoned tractors than cell towers. Four hours in the car and I hadn't seen a fast food place in the last two. I was starting to forget what drive-thru coffee looked like.

This was *literally* the middle of nowhere.

Eddie swerved suddenly, sending me shoulder-first into the passenger door of our rental SUV.

"What the hell?" I demanded, pulling myself back upright.

"There was an armadillo in the road."

I stared at him incredulously as I rubbed my bruised arm. "An *armadillo*?"

He made a face.

First a tumbleweed, and now an armadillo? Those had to be against traffic laws or something.

"How much longer?" I whined.

"According to the GPS," he said, "about twenty minutes."

I dropped my head back against the seat. "Thank God."

"Oh, my bad," he correct. "We exit the freeway in twenty minutes. It's another thirty-five after that until we're in Rocky Gulch."

If Eddie knew how badly I wanted to stab him in the neck with a pen right now, he would probably pull over and make me get out of the car.

If he knew how badly I wanted to stab myself in the neck with a pen, he would probably hand me a sharp ballpoint.

I settled for digging the bottle of antacids out of my purse and chomping two chewable cherry tablets. As much as I didn't want to *be* in the middle of nowhere, I wanted to *die* in the middle of nowhere even less.

As we chased the sun toward the horizon, I thought back over the series of events that somehow culminated in my exile to America's answer to Siberia, aka the desert dry plains of central Texas.

In my own defense, I couldn't have known. I wasn't in charge of the casting decisions, and even if I had been, I couldn't possibly have known that four of the five cast members on our gay makeover reality show, *One Straight Guy at a Time*, were in fact not gay at all. I wasn't a mind reader and my gaydar was apparently set on oblivious. How was this my fault?

Still, as the least senior producer involved, when the big boss set out the chopping block, my neck was the first one offered up in sacrifice.

I should have been grateful that Bud Gorman was giving me a second chance.

My mission was simple. If I could produce the rough pilot of a new show, *Try It On*, with a next-to-nothing budget and only a cameraman for crew, without incident, he would consider—*consider*—putting me back on the list. And the list was where I wanted to be. Where I *needed* to be. Being on the list was Plan A for climbing the ladder of career success, all the way to an Emmy, an Oscar, and a Golden Globe at the very top. Being off the list was... well, I refused to consider that possibility. There was no Plan B.

I was under no misconception that this was anything less than a sudden death probation. I *had* to make *Try It On* a success.

Try It On was one of those reality shows where seemingly normal and sane people—and I used those terms in the most liberal sense—gave up their ordinary lives to experience something completely different. Episodes in the works included a stay at home mom who would live the life of a Park Avenue princess, a school teacher who would play the part of

Broadway star, and a motorcycle shop owner who would try to hack it as a park ranger. What made *Try It On* different from the five-thousand other shows with the same general premise was the amount of time participants committed to their trial lives—an entire month.

Filed under the why-would-anyone-do-something-so-dumb category of TV shows, as far as I was concerned, but a gig was a gig and I needed to get back on Bud's good side. My career in television was ready to take off and I needed to stay on the right track.

Even if that meant I had to spend the next thirty days in exile from civilization.

"Chocolate?" Eddie asked.

"Sure." I sat up a little straighter in my seat and held out my hand. "Thanks."

He scowled at me sideways. "As in do you have any?"

"Oh." I slumped. "No. Not even a breath mint."

"My boyfriend always has chocolate." Eddie pursed his lips. "Then again, he's more of a girl than you are."

I punched him in the arm. "If I had known we were traversing the Kalahari, I would have grabbed a jumbo bag of candy bars along with my antacid."

When Bud told me I could choose my own cameraman for the pilot from the selection of lens jockeys with horse riding experience—a very necessary skill for someone expected to capture every moment of life of a working ranch—I been relieved to see Eddie Monroe on the list.

He was the size of a taxi—and not an ordinary four-passenger sedan taxi, one of the giant minivan ones reserved for swarms of tourists with more luggage than sense. He was fast as a panther, though, and had the ability to make me laugh in almost any situation, which was why I'd blurted his name on the spot.

We'd been through more disastrous productions together than I cared to remember. He saved me from a trip to the ER on *Apes with Knives*, managed to make a hardened cage fighter cry on *Into the Octagon*, and deftly avoided the advances of a dozen drunk coeds—whose gaydar was as faulty as mine—on *Spring Break Strip Poker*. On top of all that, the man was a regular Houdini with a camera.

I knew that if I was going to be stuck in the middle of nowhere for a month, the only way to make the experience bearable would be to bring along someone who knew how to get the best shots in the worst conditions and who I could actually tolerate for long periods of time.

Lord knew, there was nothing else about this wasteland that was inviting me to hang out any longer than I absolutely had to.

I popped another antacid and quietly knocked my head against the window.

♥

EDDIE STOPPED the car in front of the dusty blue Victorian house with a three-story turret and dormers in the roof. A streetlight out front cast an amber glow that turned the white trim into gold. A carved, painted sign in the yard declared this the *Yellow Rose Bunkhouse Bed and Breakfast*.

A picture-perfect image that looked straight off a movie set. Hopefully not one with a psycho serial killer hiding inside.

"Not bad," I said as I climbed out of the car. "I'll go get us checked in."

The sidewalk and front path were lined with small purple flowers with centers that were almost the same color as the house itself. When I got to the front door, I hesitated. I'd never stayed in a bed and breakfast before. It was kind of a hotel, but it looked like a house. What was the protocol for this time of night? Was I supposed to knock or just walk right in?

I tried the handle and found it unlocked.

In the end, I decided on a hybrid approach. I knocked on the door while opening it and walking inside.

"Hello?" I whisper-shouted to the empty front hall.

There was a table to the left with an open book, like a guest register. Otherwise, it looked completely residential. A pair of doorways opened off the hall to either side. One led to a dining room, with a big wooden table and a dozen mix-and-matched chairs. The other was hidden by a decorative folding screen, painted with a cattle drive scene straight out of the Wild West.

This really looked like someone's house. Maybe the sign out front was a mistake. Maybe I missed an arrow or something. I needed to get out of there before I was arrested for breaking and entering. Or at least entering.

"Welcome to the Yellow Rose Bunkhouse," a cheerful voice whispered behind me.

I covered my mouth to hold in a shriek as I spun around to find an older woman, mid-to-late-sixties probably, with a broad smile on her round face and a pile of gray hair curled into a loose bun. She wore plain blue pants and pale blue blouse beneath a brightly-colored floral apron.

Blue seemed to be the color of the day—or night, as it were.

"Can I help you?" she asked, her smile unwavering.

"I'm Cassie Bishop," I replied, keeping my voice as low as hers. I stepped forward and offered her my hand. "I'm with Go Gorman Studios."

Her head tilted slightly to one side and her smile grew twice as big. She stepped forward, bypassing my offered hand to pull me into a tight hug.

"It's so nice to meet you, Cassie," she said as she patted me on the back. "I'm Sue-Anne Arnold. I'm the chief cook and bottle-washer here."

"It's a beautiful…" I struggled to choose the right word. Hotel? House? Bed and breakfast? I decided to avoid the confusion altogether. "It's beautiful."

"Did you just come by to check out the property?" she asked.

Property! That was appropriately neutral.

"No, we're ready to check in."

Her eyes widened and for some reason that made my heart beat a little faster.

"I'm sorry, but—" She wrung her hands helplessly. "—we have no vacancy tonight. The Filcher-Farmer wedding is next weekend and they have the entire place booked. We're full."

"Full?" She couldn't be serious. "We have a reservation."

"Yes," she replied. "For next month."

"For next—?" I shook my head. "No, that's not possible."

She gestured at me to follow her and then turned and walked deeper into the house. We went down the hallway, past the staircase, through an open doorway, and into a cozy white kitchen. Sue-Anne crossed to the round kitchen table where a laptop was open. She sat down and started punching in keys.

A moment later, she called me over.

"Here, look," she said pointing at the screen.

I leaned down to read the open email from Bud's assistant, Marian, making the arrangements for our reservations. The date in the original email was one month off.

That was just what I wanted to hear after a long day of travel. I got up a four o'clock this morning to finish packing and had been trying to get to the middle of Texas—Rocky Gulch, to be exact—ever since.

First, our itinerary indicated a flight out of LaGuardia, only to get there and be told we were flying out of Newark. One high-speed cab ride later, we arrived just as the flight was canceled. After being bumped from three flights—thanks to awful thunderstorms blanketing the Midwest—we finally got routed through Atlanta, Chicago, and Denver, before catching the last flight into Dallas.

What should have been a short, direct flight had turned into an all-day mess.

It was after midnight back in New York.

Exhaustion and frustration hit me full force.

I shoved a hand into my curls. "Crap."

"Language dear," she said gently.

Fine, there had to be another option. We would just have to find another place to stay.

"Sorry," I offered lamely. "It's been a long day. Can you recommend another place to stay in town?"

Her laugh tinkled like bells on a Christmas tree. "There isn't one."

I scowled. She couldn't be serious.

"I'm sorry, but Rocky Gulch isn't terribly metropolitan. The

Yellow Rose is the only lodging in town." At least she sounded genuinely sorry. "If I had a cot or a bedroll to spare I'd make room. Even the sofas in the parlor are full of little ones tonight."

I sighed. "How far is the next closest hotel?"

"That'd be two exits down on the highway," she offered. "Near to an hour away I'd imagine."

"An hour?" I couldn't hide my shock.

How was it possible that the closest thing to a hotel in this town was full *and* the next closest place to stay was over an hour away?

This production was already a nightmare, and filming hadn't even started.

"I'm so sorry, dear." She reached out and patted my hand.

I took a deep breath and let it out very slowly. "It's fine. We'll make it work."

She pushed to her feet and crossed to the counter, where a rack full of freshly-baked treats sat cooling. She placed a pair of muffins at the center of a blue bandana and then wrapped them up. Tied them with a bow and everything.

"Here," she said, handing me the bundle, "take these for the road."

I gave her a weak smile. "Thanks."

Sue-Anne followed me to the front door and waved as I climbed back into the rental car. As soon as the door clicked shut, I let out a string of sailor-worthy swear words.

Eddie stared at me. He wasn't entirely unused to this kind of rant from me, but usually it took at least a couple days of shooting for something to so completely upend my calm.

Today I was ahead of the curve.

When I finished, he cleared his throat. "How'd it go?"

I glared at him. "Bud's idiot assistant reserved the wrong dates."

Marian tried hard. At least, I thought she tried hard. Maybe she was just really good at pretending to try hard. Clearly she was *not* good at actual work.

On any production you have to roll with the punches. Avoidable punches are a little more painful to swallow.

"So, let me guess," he said. "No room at the inn?"

"There's a wedding this weekend." I forced my fists to unclench. "The entire bed and breakfast is full and the next closest hotel is an hour away, back on the freeway."

Eddie shook his head. Then sniffed the air. "Do I smell blueberries?"

I handed him the muffin bundle. If he could be appeased by a pair of muffins, who was I to deny him?

Letting my head drop back against the seat, I considered our options.

Choice one, we drive *all* the way back to the hotel on the freeway. But even if they had rooms available—clearly not a sure thing, given my current luck—we would have to drive *all* the way back here in the morning. The shoot was scheduled to begin a seven, which would mean getting up at the butt-crack of dawn. Again.

I groaned at the thought. It was already nearly midnight. If I didn't get a good night's sleep, things could get ugly.

"These are amazing," Eddie exclaimed. He held out a muffin to me. "You sure you don't want one?"

I shook my head. All I wanted was sleep.

Choice two, we… what? Stayed here?

I twisted around in my seat. The car rental company had upgraded us to a full-size SUV. The thing was a least a few square feet larger than my apartment. The passenger seat felt like a luxurious recliner and the back seat looked like a darn comfy sofa bed.

"Hey Eddie," I asked, "how would you feel about spending a night in the car?"

TWO

"HERE COMES YOUR COWBOY," Eddie said.

I turned away from studying the small group of horses gathered at the fence line and saw a cloud of dust rising up from the road that led to our location. If you could even call that unpaved strip of dirt and gravel a *road*. I heard the truck long before I could actually see it, its engine roaring like the subway outside my apartment.

What I wouldn't have given to be back in the city.

As I watched, the amber glow of the early morning sun hit the dust storm and turned it into a swirl of gold. Too bad we hadn't caught that on tape. I made a mental note to add that to the shot list for tomorrow.

The truck ground to a halt half a city block away, at the far the end of a weather-beaten building that looked more like a piece of modern art than a functioning structure. The truck might have looked even worse—I couldn't tell under the thick layer of red-brown mud that covered every surface. It had double wheels on the rear axle and an extended cab, so it couldn't have been too ancient. The windows appeared clean, but the reflection of the rising sun created a mirrored sunglasses effect, so I couldn't see the cowboy inside.

Several of the horses whinnied, leaning out over the fence, toward the now silent truck. I watched just as eagerly as the driver's side door swung open.

When Bud first gave me the rundown on the pilot episode, I imagined cowgirl trainer Ty Haywood to be a short, middle-aged man with a big beer belly and an even bigger cowboy hat who wore a plaid western shirt with pearly buttons, too-tight dark blue jeans, and an ostentatious belt buckle and who said things like *yes ma'am* and drank sweet tea by the bucket.

The picture in the dossier had been hard to make out, like it was taken at a distance and then blown up. Or like he hadn't known the picture was being taken. It showed the cowboy, sitting on a horse and looking out over the range, or something ranchy like that. Too grainy to make out any real details.

I imagined the casting department had better pictures and probably video from the audition process, but if they did they weren't sharing with me.

I watched as first one and then a second cowboy boot stomped to the ground beneath the open door. They were as dusty as the truck. Unlike the shiny, pointy-toed ones I'd expected—with fancy stitching and exotic leather—they looked more like beaten up work boots.

And the pale blue jeans that hung down over them looked just as worn, dusty and broken in. A little frayed along the hem. They hit the boot exactly right, wrinkling up a bit in the front and stopping right above the ground in the back.

The hand that gripped the door frame was my first clue that maybe I'd watched too much *Storage Wars: Texas* as research. It was strong and tan and clearly used to long hours of hard work.

I sucked in a tight breath.

The strong, tan, hard-working hand slammed the door shut and I got my first view of the attached cowboy.

Eddie let out a low whistle.

The cowboy was pretty much the opposite of everything I had imagined. He was around my age—early to mid-thirties. He was tall, at least six foot. Those faded jeans he wore hugged him in all the right places and the blue-gray tee on top did the same. There wasn't a belt, buckle, or belly in sight. And instead of a cowboy hat, he wore a baseball cap.

Even from this distance I could make out the team logo.

Right there, in the middle of the Texas outback and on the head of possibly the most gorgeous guy I'd ever seen in real life—and I'd seen a lot—was a pristine white NY embroidered on a navy blue hat. The cowboy was a Yankees fan.

I almost swooned on the spot.

"Cassie?"

I dragged my attention away from the cowboy, turning to the sound of my name. Climbing out of the passenger side of the truck was a woman. A blond woman. A *beautiful* blond woman.

Reality slapped me in the face. *Of course* a guy that hot wasn't single. I mentally flipped to the second page of the dossier, to one Genevieve Haywood, co-owner of the Black Willow Ranch. They probably had six kids at home. What twilight zone did I think I was in?

At least that would make things easier. For a moment there I'd had trouble breathing. Couldn't film if I couldn't breathe.

"Yes," I said, trying not to let my shoulders slump as my heart rate returned to normal. "I'm Cassie Bishop."

"I'm Genevieve, co-owner, marketing manager, and a whole lot of other things here a Black Willow Ranch." She lifted a hand to shield her eyes from the bright sun. "I'm the one who arranged this whole thing. I've been exchanging emails with your boss for months."

Her voice had a gentle lilt that reminded me a bit of my best friend Bethany's southern drawl. As Genevieve rounded the front of the truck, I tried not to envy her petite curves and infectious smile. Wearing skinny jeans tucked into knee-high boots and a three-quarter sleeve denim jacket layered over a maroon tank, she would fit in on a Hollywood movie set as easily as she seemed to belong in the wilds of Texas.

In my black jeans, black tee, black cardigan, and black boots I must have looked like a walking poster for New York City style. I didn't fit in anywhere else.

"Mr. Gorman told me all about you," Genevieve continued.

She hooked her arm around the cowboy's bicep.

"And this is Ty," she said, beaming with pride as she leaned playfully into his side. "Your future TV star—"

Was he blushing under that Yankees cap?

"—and my big brother."

"What?" I snapped before I could stop myself.

Eddie snorted.

I cut the cameraman a sharp glare and he pretended not to notice.

Genevieve was the cowboy's little sister. That explained the adoring look and—now that I thought about it—the family resemblance. My heart rate sped right back up.

"Nice to meet you Genevieve," I said, ignoring my

suddenly out-of-control hormones. I even managed to look right into the cowboy's bright blue eyes as I nodded at him. "Ty. I'm the field producer for *Try It On*."

Then I couldn't seem to tear my gaze *away* from those baby blues. It didn't help that he stepped forward and held out his hand.

"A pleasure," he said, his voice deep and smooth. "I look forward to working with you, Cassie."

My knees might have buckled a little as he said my name.

Get a grip! Seriously, this job was too important to get all melty inside over the super-hot star of the show. I should have been focusing on how great he would look on camera. Our target demographic—female viewers ages twenty-five to forty-five—were going to go nuts over his full lips and sculpted features. They would write poems about his blindingly white smile. I flicked a barely-there glance at his left ring finger. Yep, the studio would get mail by the truckload asking the cowboy to date them, marry them, or just father their children.

Heck, I was smack dab in the middle of the target demographic and I could barely think straight. He would make the show an instant hit.

As long as I didn't screw it up first.

I boldly took his offered hand.

It was just as rough and warm and hard-working as I imagined. The heat from his touch shot straight down my spine. All the way to my unpolished toes.

I yanked my hand away before the sensation completely dissolved my judgment.

"And this is Eddie—" I stammered, pointing at the big guy. "Cameraman."

"Just pretend I'm not here," he grumbled.

I shot him a sarcastic grin. "I try and I try."

"Don't piss off the guy with the camera." He tapped at the device he kept practically glued to his shoulder. "I can make ten on-air pounds look like twenty."

Eddie might have been a grouch, but he was great at his job and I actually understood his humor. We were a good team.

"Well it sure is a pleasure to have y'all here at the ranch," Genevieve said, ignoring—or oblivious to—our exchange. "I'm sure you're eager to get started."

I nodded. "As soon as the other half of the cast shows up," I said. "Eddie and I will do some scouting until she gets here."

Then, once the starlet-wannabe arrived, the real action would begin.

♥

"WHAT DO you mean *she's not coming*?" I barked into the phone.

If my voice rose to a slightly higher pitch than usual—verging on canines-only range—I wasn't surprised. I had a good reason. Anyone in my position would have the same reaction. Shock-induced fury.

I turned and walked a few paces away from the cast and crew—which, right then, consisted of Eddie, Ty and Genevieve, several horses, and a fat orange cat—and said, "You tell her she either gets her designer princess butt down here right now or I will personally sue her for breach of contract and—"

The line went dead and, after three loud beeps to let me know the call had ended, I heard only silence. I glared at my phone. That douche hung up on me.

When my phone rang, my first thought had been over-whelming joy that there actually was cell signal to be had in this uncivilized wasteland. Maybe there was hope for the next thirty days after all. Then I answered, and all joy left the state.

I punched the callback button and listened impatiently as the phone rang. And rang and rang and finally went to voicemail.

"This is Vince. Leave a message. I'll get back to you."

I tried three more times with the same result.

Yep, definitely being punished. Big time.

Was it possible to telepathically kill someone halfway around the world? If it wasn't, it should have been. And I should have been the first one given that power.

"Problem Cass?"

I dreaded turning around to face Eddie.

Above all else, a producer has to exude confidence. Certainty. The absolute belief that everything was going to work out, no matter how much in the toilet the situation seemed at the moment.

That particular bit of optimism was beyond me at the moment.

I chomped my lips together and dragged in a confidence-building breath. Dust filled the air and, now, my lungs. I started hacking so hard that Eddie pounded on my back.

"Th-thanks," I said between coughs, trying to recover the air he'd knocked out of my chest. I dug out an antacid and took a moment to chew and swallow the chalky cherry relief. Sucking it up, I straightened my spine and turned to face him. "The merry princess isn't coming."

Now, Eddie might have looked like a bear—big, broad, and scruffy-faced—but he was normally as sweet as Bethany's world famous pecan pie. Heck, he nearly killed us both to save an armadillo on the highway yesterday. He was soft as wet cotton candy on the inside. So when he let out a string of expletives, I knew I wasn't exaggerating the situation.

"You know what happens if you tank this shoot?" he asked.

I gave him a humorless look. Of course I knew. Bye bye, Cassie Bishop, production manager. Hello, Cassie Bishop, you want fries with that?

"If I don't shoot this pilot, on time and on budget," I replied, sliding my hands into the back pocket of my jeans, which were now more dusty red than black, "I'm toast."

Eddie nodded. I hadn't told him about my do-or-die probation, but he knew anyway. Everyone at the entire production company—if not the entire television industry—probably knew. A girl going down in flames made the best gossip.

I would not let myself crack under the pressure.

Think, Cassie. Think.

The pilot episode was meant to star a Hollywood trust fund diva—Bud's wife's cousin's niece or something ridiculously nepotistic like that—spending a month learning how to be a cowgirl. Like, a real life, riding the range and roping the cattle cowgirl.

It was, supposedly, her lifelong dream.

According to the little brat's patronizing agent—the aforementioned douche Vince who just hung up on me—she was currently sunbathing in the south of France with no intention of visiting the Lone Star state anytime ever. Which left me short one trust fund diva and on the verge of a total career disaster.

Oh God, I was going to have to call Bud and tell him. I was going to have to apologize for something that wasn't my fault and beg for more time, just long enough to get a replacement from… somewhere.

My ears already burned in anticipation of the tongue-lashing he would unleash. A delay on the first day was not the way to get back in his good graces.

I jammed my fingers into my black curls. There had to be another way. It didn't have to be *that* particular spoiled rich girl. Weren't they all pretty much the same? Surely I could find another.

Maybe it didn't even have to be an actual spoiled rich girl at all. Really, it only needed to be someone whose life was the complete opposite of life on a Texas ranch. I knew plenty of girls who fit that bill. Some of whom might even want to be on TV.

Maybe I could call Bethany.

No dice. My best friend was busy making her boutique work and exchanging googly eyes with her new boyfriend, Chris, one of the previously mentioned non-gay cast members of my last production. I'd gotten her the gig working on the show, so I could hardly begrudge her having found love in the process.

All my friends from college were either climbing corporate ranks or raising a pack of babies. All my friends from film school, the ones who hadn't given up on the industry altogether and fallen off the face of the planet, were hard at work on their own careers.

From the moment the plane—finally—took off from Newark yesterday morning, I had a bad feeling about this job.

Shoot, I knew this was trouble from the moment Bud called me into his office and offered me this probation deal. I had no choice but to accept, even though country life would be pure torture for a city girl like me.

Well, I wouldn't let it all go to waste. If I was going to salvage this opportunity, I had to think fast. I had to think big. Nothing-left-to-lose big.

My stomach plummeted. Oh God.

No, I tried to tell my brain. *This is not a good idea. This is a terrible idea, even.*

But my brain wouldn't listen. It had one idea and one idea only.

"Roll tape," I barked at Eddie as I reached into my multi-function cross-body bag. "And play along."

He shrugged and lifted the camera onto his shoulder. It wasn't like *his* career was on the line here. Just mine.

And I was not about to let some spoiled brat derail me.

After sifting through the contents of my bag—wallet, smartphone, an emergency supply of Xanax for nervous actors, my ever-present bottle of antacids, and a handful of pilfered peppermints I grabbed after dinner the other night—I finally found the two things I was looking for.

Pulling out the hair band, I swiped my fingers through my hair and hastily shoved my curls into a high ponytail. Then, for the first time since Bethany started making me carry it in college, I actually used her girlmergency secret weapon.

I flipped open the all-over-color compact, rubbed my fingers into the deep peachy-rose shade, and dotted the cream onto my cheeks, lips, and eyelids. A quick glance in the tiny mirror confirmed Bethany's promise that it would instantly turn even a makeup-hating, all-black-wearing New Yorker into a girly-girl.

"I can do this," I muttered as I stuffed the compact back into my bag.

In my last moments of sanity, I wracked my brain for any option other than the one desperation had given me. But short of running away to Mexico—too much spicy food—or calling Bud to tell him what happened—too much career suicide—this was it.

"Are we still waiting for the, um… cowgirl in training?" Genevieve asked.

My spine stiffened.

"If we are, we'll be waiting a long time," I muttered.

"I beg your pardon?" she replied with a puzzled smile.

"Actually, no." This was ridiculous. The fear of losing my career must have been affecting the decision-making parts of my brain. Normal, rational Cassie could never do something so insane. I shook my head, regretting my words even as I said them. "There's been a change of plans."

I sensed Eddie turn the camera on me. Clever bastard knew what I was going to do.

I forced a tight smile.

"*I* will be playing the part of cowgirl wannabe."

Eddie choked. Or coughed. Or choke-coughed.

Ty's eyebrows lifted beneath his Yankees brim.

Genevieve clapped her hands together and bounded toward me. "That's wonderful!"

I might have jerked away as she wrapped her arms around me, engulfing me in a tight hug, but she didn't seem to notice. My pleading look in Eddie's direction went unnoticed—or ignored.

"This is going to be so much fun," she squealed in my ear.

"Come on, Cassie Bishop," Ty said. "Let's go meet your horse."

"Horse?" I choked.

What had I done?

THREE

"HOLD ON," I said, trying to buy myself some time. "We need to, um, go over procedures and shooting schedules and segment plans before we get to, you know… *horses*."

Ty laughed—a deep, knee-buckling laugh—and turned back to face me. "Don't tell me you're afraid of horses."

I threw a sideways glare at Eddie, who was laughing *and* getting it all on tape.

Only Genevieve managed to keep a straight face.

"I'm not afraid…" I insisted. "I've just never met one before."

In New York, there weren't many ways to get up close and personal with a horse. You could take pricey riding lessons at one of the few stables left in the city—which I hadn't. You could take a carriage ride through Central Park—a favorite pastime of gawking tourists, but not life-long residents. Or you could chat up one of the mounted police officers from the NYPD—not exactly a recommended activity.

So, no, I'd never met a horse.

"Don't worry," Ty said, walking backward toward the

fence line full of horses. "Roughshod is the sweetest mare we've got. She'll be gentle with you."

"Roughshod?" I whispered. "Doesn't sound sweet."

Genevieve moved to my side.

"Ty is magical with horses." She looped her arm through mine and started walking me closer to the horses. "I think he keeps sugar cubes in his pockets. They make moon eyes at him whenever he walks by."

As Genevieve led me across the gravel driveway, I watched in awe as Ty walked up to the fence and the horses jockeyed to get closest to him. He patted them on their noses and they snickered in return. Such big, scary creatures acting like gentle puppies.

Then again, if Ty offered me some sugar every day, I would make moon eyes at him too. Which was exactly the wrong thought to have, considering how closely I was going to be working with him for the next month. Ty's role on the show was to be the mentor to the cowgirl-in-training. He was responsible for teaching her everything she needed to know to become as close to a real-life cowgirl as possible. That meant long hours and close quarters.

If I was going to spend those long hours admiring the way his jeans hugged his backside—not that I was doing that or anything—then it was going to make for either very awkward situations or very boring television. Probably both.

I tried to shake myself out of it. Really I did.

Then, in one fluid movement, Ty placed his hand on the top rail, lifted one foot to the middle one, and launched himself over the fence and into the pen.

I sucked in a sharp breath.

"Has that effect on the ladies, too," Genevieve added. She called out, "Show off!"

I bit my lips to keep from saying anything that might indicate that I'd been having that very reaction since the moment I laid eyes on him.

"I keep trying to get him to pick one and settle down." She clucked, like a despairing mother, even though she was clearly a few years younger than Ty. "A lady, I mean. I'm ready to be an auntie. But working fifteen- to eighteen-hour days doesn't leave much time for dating."

Her voice grew quieter the closer we got to Ty, like she didn't want him to hear.

Which didn't explain why she was telling *me*. We'd only met three minutes ago, and already she was confiding family secrets. Then again—I glanced around at the vast empty nothing around us—maybe open ears were few and far between out here.

When we reached the fence, all my thoughts and questions fled. Genevieve released my arm and I stood there with nothing more than a few pieces of weathered wood separating me from the horses.

Ty had his arm hugged around the neck of a yellow horse. The beast was huge—although, in comparison, it was not quite as tall as Ty and not nearly as big as the rest of the horses. Frozen to the spot, I watched as he whispered soothing words and led it over to me.

"Cassie, this is Roughshod," he said, patting the horse on the neck. "She's a sweet old thing. Roughshod, this is Cassie. She'll be riding you for the next few weeks."

Few weeks? I almost fainted.

As if the horse understood, she leaned forward and sniffed

at my hands where they held the fence rail in a death grip. The soft velvet of her nose tickled over my fingertips. Hot breath puffed out a second before she opened her lips and—

"Aaack!" I screamed and jumped back, knocking into Eddie who was capturing every last terror-filled moment.

The horse nickered softly as Ty soothed her. "Shhh, it's alright. Just startled her is all."

"She was going to bite me," I accused.

"Roughshod? Nah." Ty gave me a lopsided smile, the dimple in one cheek deeper than the other. "She was only feeling you out."

He waved me back up to the fence.

I shook my head desperately. "Shooting schedules," I stammered, "and segment plans and—"

"Come on," Ty insisted. "Just meet her."

The warm look in his bright blue eyes overrode my fear and, as much as my every instinct screamed to turn and run away, I cautiously inched forward. He held out his hand and, with warning bells clanging in my mind, I took it.

Between the feel of his hand wrapped around mine and the fear of the crazy beast in front of me, it was amazing I stayed upright. My heart pounded like a jackhammer. I wobbled a little, but locked my knees and forced myself not to faint or fall over. Somehow I managed, and I let Ty guide my hand toward Roughshod's mouth.

"Keep your palm flat," he said softly.

The horse sniffed my fingers and when she tried to nibble again Ty held fast and kept my hand in place.

Only abject terror kept me silent.

"Shhh," he whispered.

Roughshod moved her lips over my skin, as if using them

to feel in place of fingers. Her touch was so soft it almost tick-led. After a thorough exploration, she sputtered hot air on my palm and then moved away.

She dropped her head and reached for a tiny patch of grass just out of chomping range on the other side of the fence.

"Wow," I said, because there were no other words.

"Told ya," Ty replied.

I looked at him—his blue eyes sparkling and twin dimples accenting his smile, his hand still enveloping mine—and I felt it. Every nerve ending in my body felt it. That punch in the gut that told me I was in deep, deep trouble. Texas-sized trouble.

"See, nothing to be afraid of," Genevieve said as she stepped up to my side.

Her voice yanked me out of the moment.

I broke the hypnotizing eye contact, pulled my hand away, and turned to her.

"You're right," I said, louder than necessary. "She's a big teddy bear."

Genevieve's blue eyes—a slightly darker shade than her brother's—studied me for a moment, then shifted to Ty. When she settled back on me there was a spark of mischief in her eye.

That way lay danger. I had to change the direction of this runaway train—fast.

"So, now that we've done the introductions," I blurted, "Eddie and I need to go check into our rooms at the hotel back out on the highway."

As in I needed to get as far away from this horse—and the strange heat that filled my chest when I looked Ty straight in the eye—as quickly as possible.

"The Galloping Inn?" Genevieve asked.

Ty frowned. "That's an hour away."

I huffed out an irritated sigh. "Don't I know it. But apparently the only lodging in Rocky Gulch is booked up through the weekend."

We would lose a lot of time in the daily commute. But we would make it work. If Eddie drove, I could draft shooting plans and write my daily reports for Bud on the way here and back. It would be fine.

"Oh that's right," Genevieve said with an apologetic grimace. "The Filcher-Farmer wedding. I never even thought about that."

"It's no big deal," I replied. "I called this morning and made a reservation. We're all set."

"Don't be silly," Genevieve said, shushing me. "That's a waste of time and gas money."

"Good thing I have an expense account," I joked.

"Nonsense, you'll do no such thing." She pursed her lips in a determined smirk. "We have plenty of room."

"Room?" I echoed.

She grinned like a Cheshire cat—and I felt like a big, juicy canary.

"Absolutely," she insisted. "You two will stay at the ranch. With us."

Eddie shifted his weight.

Ty coughed.

I closed my eyes. This was going to be bad.

♥

"THIS IS STUPID, RIGHT?" I asked Eddie.

My grip on the steering wheel tightened as I followed the dirt-covered truck down the gravel road. It's wheels sputtered dust up into the air, coating our rental in a thick layer of that same red-brown that painted the truck.

According to Genevieve, they had a couple of empty guest rooms in the main house that they reserved for family and special guests. Normally I made it policy to keep cast and crew separate on location—it kept things simpler, made interpersonal conflicts less likely. But in this case, the line between cast and crew was as fuzzy as a year-old bagel. I was walking both sides of the lens on this production. And the idea of saving two hours of driving time each day made me almost giddy to accept her offer.

Now that our lodging was settled and we were on our way to the main house, I had time to think back over my decision. My ridiculous and impulsive decision. Was I really going to play the cowgirl wannabe?

When Eddie didn't respond to my question I turned to glare at him—what, like I was going to drive off the road and into a tumbleweed?

I found myself staring into my own reflection, distorted by the camera lens.

I clenched my teeth. "Turn it off."

"This is good stuff," he insisted, not following my orders.

"Turn. It. *Off.*"

With a dramatic sigh, he lifted the camera off his shoulder and set it in his lap. I glanced over to make sure he had actually turned it off. It only takes one candid video on YouTube to make a girl permanently paranoid about being recorded off the record.

"It's not stupid," he said. "Crazy? Yes. But not stupid."

"Viewers will never know." I wasn't sure if I was convincing him or myself. "We'll use the intro to establish me as a dyed-in-the-wool city girl who has always longed to try the cowgirl life."

I almost choked on my own words.

"Have you?" Eddie asked.

I didn't bother responding.

"I can juggle like a master, but you'll have to cover some of my duties." The SUV hit a rough spot, knocking me against the door. "When I'm on camera—" On camera? I could *not* believe I was actually going to do this. "—you need to make shooting decisions and make sure things roll smoothly off screen."

"Don't worry," Eddie said. "We'll make it work."

If it were any other cameraman, I wouldn't even consider it. I was a bit of a control freak—okay, a *lot* of a control freak—and the very thought of handing over some of my production duties to someone else made my neck itch. I reached for my bag and forced a tight smile when Eddie pressed my bottle of antacids into my hand. If anyone could step in and—with my never-too-far-away guidance—take my place, he could.

I would still direct the main action, still process the dailies, and still send the regular reports to Bud. Probation wasn't without its paperwork.

Who knows? Maybe one day I would look back on this experience with fondness and gratitude. That day was probably far, far in the future, but it could happen.

Off to the left, a little ways down the road, I could see the house. It was actually within walking distance of the barn, via narrow footpath, but by car we'd had to drive halfway around the county to get from one to the other.

I wasn't sure what I expected the house to look like, maybe something one story with lots of wood and sweeping views of bucolic pasture, but this was a far cry from anything I might have imagined.

The square-shaped building stood two stories tall with a porch spanning the front side. The entire thing was made of stones. Big stones, little stones, beige to brown and every shade in between. The second story had three small windows that peeked out over the roof of the inviting porch—with the requisite idyllic swing at one end.

There was a certain… gentleness about it.

Eddie lifted the camera back onto his shoulder and filmed our arrival.

I pulled in next to the truck and cut the engine. For a moment—a *long* moment—I considered not getting out. Quitting would be so much easier. The list of reasons to give up and go home scrolled through my mind like closing credits. But as ridiculous and, okay, *scary* as this whole thing was, it was also a means to an end. Save the show, save my career.

Like I had another choice. Actors were always talking about motivation. Well, I had mine in spades.

Shoving the last of my reservations aside, I opened the door.

Before I could set one foot on the ground, a massive weight thudded into my shoulder and knocked me sideways toward the passenger seat.

"Babe!" Ty shouted. "Get off her!"

Something wet smeared over my ear. I screamed.

Then, suddenly, the weight was gone.

I looked up and saw Ty holding a massive black… *thing* by the collar.

"Bad dog," he said in a stern voice. "No jumping on visitors."

"That's a *dog*?" I demanded. It looked more like a bear.

The black thing stood up on two legs, placing a pair of massive paws on Ty's shoulders. They were almost the same height.

"This is Babe," Ty said with a laugh as the dog tried to lick his face. "She's a Bull Mastiff-Newfie mix."

"Tyson James Haywood." Genevieve stared at her brother, eyes wide with shock. "Did your dog attack our guest?"

"She means well." He pushed at the beast's chest and—amazingly—it dropped back down to all fours. "She gets overexcited is all."

He snapped his fingers and the dog sat.

Then Ty stepped toward me, his hand moving like he was going to offer to help me out of the car. Still a little off-kilt after the last time our hands touched, I hurried to push myself to my feet.

"It's fine," I said. "No damage."

A flash of movement in my peripheral vision told me Eddie had caught every last moment on tape. Perfect.

"Come on," Genevieve said, "let's get your things and get you settled."

Yes, let's.

I slammed the door shut, popped the rear door, and walked around to pull out my carry-on suitcase. A decade of work-related travel had trained me well. I could live pretty much indefinitely out of a small bag, provided I had access to laundry once a week and the climate extremes were moderate.

Ty reached past me and grabbed the giant black duffle. "Let me help you with that."

"Oh, that's not mine," I said, sliding my cameraman a cheeky look. "That's all Eddie's."

He blew me a mocking kiss.

I held up my carry-on. "This is me."

From the look of surprise on Ty's face, I'd say I impressed him.

Genevieve, on the other hand, despaired, "That's all you have?'

"Yes," I said proudly. "I'm a low-maintenance traveler."

She shook her head. "I bet we're about the same size," she said, studying my frame. "You can raid my closet."

"That won't be necessary," I insisted. "I have everything I need."

With a shrug that clearly said she questioned my mental state, Genevieve turned and headed toward the house. Babe and Ty followed close on her heels.

"I'll be in shortly," I said as I pulled my phone out of my purse. "I just need to call New York and check in. Let them know we arrived safely and where we're staying."

I waited until everyone had stepped inside and then walked a few paces away to dial Bud's office. But when I hit the call button, I was met with the annoying sound of a dropped call. A quick check of the signal meter on my phone showed… nothing. I'd had one measly bar over by the barn, but not even a blip now.

I pocketed my phone and headed inside. I found Genevieve and Eddie in the kitchen. She was pouring four big glasses of lemonade and he was waving a light meter around the room to see if we would need to set up extra lighting. If the echo of footsteps on the ceiling were any indication, Ty had taken our luggage upstairs.

"I have no signal," I announced.

"That's weird," Eddie said, holding the light meter up to the window. "I have two bars."

"You must have Epic Cellular," Genevieve said. "Their service is awful spotty out here. You can use the landline."

"A landline?"

I didn't know anyone who had a landline anymore. I hadn't had one in years.

Eddie picked up the camera and started filming.

I stared straight into the camera and asked, "How many days until we return to civilization?"

"Twenty-seven," Eddie said, though I couldn't tell if he was laughing or sympathizing. "Twenty-seven days."

Surely I could endure anything for seventeen days. Even no cell signal.

FOUR

WHEN MY EYES popped open the world was still dark. I squinted out into the night and wondered why I was wide awake. My hand reached blindly for the phone on my nightstand.

I lifted it into view and pressed the button.

4:47 a.m.

With a groan, I dropped my hand back on the bed. What was I doing awake this early? It wasn't even late enough back home to get up, so I had no excuse.

Then I heard it. A faint, distant noise that sounded like a cross between a dog bark and a human scream. Great. Was the house surrounded by angry wolves or something?

Since there was nothing I could do if we were—fighting off wild animals was definitely *not* in the job description—I tried to give into my aching body's desire to go back to sleep. Maybe if I just stayed still with my eyes closed for long enough I would eventually drift back away...

The sound echoed through the room again.

"Hrmph."

My body might have been exhausted, but my mind was on freaking high alert.

I gave it a few more minutes—a few more anguished stretches of uncomfortable silence—before I gave up. The sound hadn't recurred, but the damage was done. I swung my feet out of bed and padded across the cool wood floor to the corner chair where I'd flung my backpack last night.

I lifted the bag onto my shoulder and made my way as quietly as possible through the creaking house. After a quick stop in the front hall to dig yesterday's memory cards out of Eddie's camera bag, I headed for the kitchen and set myself up at the table.

Part of my job was to review the previous day's shooting and send dailies back to Bud. He didn't trust me to know what made good TV anymore and he wanted to keep tabs on me.

That was fine. It added more work to my schedule, but if this was what it took to get back in the game, I'd do it.

As the video started playing on my laptop, the hardest part was getting over the fact that *I* was on screen. I chose to be behind the scenes for a reason. I didn't want the limelight, I didn't want visible fame and I didn't get off on audience response like actors did. I just wanted to make it all happen.

I remembered the moment I knew I wanted to be involved in film and television. My freshman year at Columbia I'd taken a film history class. I thought it would be a nice light spot on my otherwise heavy class load.

We could earn extra credit for working on a student film project, so I signed up.

From the first clack of the slate, I'd been hypnotized. Seeing and experiencing firsthand all the behind-the-camera work that went into making the on-screen stuff happen was a revelation.

I declared myself a film major the next day.

Over the years of undergrad and film school, I'd had to be on screen more than once. But I was always more concerned about the camera angles and scene continuity than I was about my lines or connecting to the other actors in the scene.

I was meant to be behind-the-scenes, but sometimes you had to be on-screen to make it work.

I popped an antacid and chewed as I sped through yesterday's film, selecting out a few choice moments to send to New York. By the time I had the sample clip done, I'd downed three cherry tablets and the kitchen was full of early dawn sun.

I clicked the wireless icon in my taskbar and pulled up the list of available networks.

Looking for networks…

None came up.

I sighed. Apparently Casa Haywood wasn't set up for wi-fi. For all I knew, they didn't even have an internet connection.

Tethering to my phone was obviously not an option—I was going to have a serious chat with my mobile provider when I got back to the real world. Luckily my field production kit included a broadband modem that was purported to work anywhere there was a cell tower in range. Everyone else seemed to have signal at the house, which meant there had to be a tower somewhere around. Not the fastest data network ever, but it would have to do.

Moments later, I had my laptop connected to the two-bar signal and the clip was sending—very, very slowly—to New York.

While the video transmitted, I transferred the rest of the

files to the massive backup external drive and then slid the memory cards back into Eddie's case.

My work done, I finally looked up from the computer. And saw Genevieve standing in the kitchen.

"Good morning," she chirped when she saw me looking at her.

"Morning," I replied. "I didn't see you come in."

She crossed her arms over her chest and smiled. "You were so focused on your work, I didn't want to disturb you."

I checked the status on my message—seven percent. *Sigh.*

"Can I help?" I offered, pushing away from the table.

"You sit your behind back down," she chided. "You have enough work ahead of you today. By tonight you'll be thanking me for the rest."

She turned back to the stove, and I dutifully sank into my chair. It only took a few moments to get antsy. I didn't like sitting around doing nothing, especially not when there was work to be done. Just watching Genevieve heat up a skillet on the stove and whisk eggs in a bowl made me itch.

By the time Eddie walked in a few minutes later I was on the verge of leaping to my feet and diving in.

He stretched his arms out wide like a grizzly waking from a long winter's sleep, camera clutched tightly in one big paw, yawning and half-growling something that sounded like *Good morning,* but I couldn't be sure. The smile on his face, however, was unmistakable.

I scowled at him. "Why are you so chipper?"

"Fresh air." He shrugged. "Makes me sleep like a baby."

My head throbbed and the rising sun was way too bright considering how little I slept the night before. The bed had been comfortable—if a little squeaky—and I was exhausted when I finally crawled between the sheets. But my mind had been racing. Running through lists of shots and setups, props, plots, and plans. Checking, double checking, and triple checking all my to-do lists, just to make sure that nothing got missed.

There was a lot riding on the success of this pilot. I couldn't let anything fall through the cracks.

I rubbed at my temples, wondering if this was what caffeine withdrawal felt like. My last coffee had been at the airport day before yesterday.

Eddie set up his camera on the counter, angled at the table. He punched the record button and the red filming light came on as he took a chair at the opposite end—presumably just outside the frame of his shot.

"I hope you like scrambled eggs," Genevieve said as she carried her skillet over from the stove. "Ty says I make the best in five counties."

She started heaping a pile of fluffy yellow onto my plate before I could say a word. Lucky for us both, I loved scrambled eggs.

The Haywood family kitchen looked like something out of a vintage issue of Better Homes and Gardens. Floral wallpaper, painted cabinets, and hardwood floors. The walls were covered with memorabilia—tin stars and embroidery samplers and framed pictures. A huge collection of magnets decorated the refrigerator and sunny yellow curtains framed the window above the sink.

"I like anything that goes in my mouth," Eddie said, holding up his plate.

"See how I'm just letting that perfect setup go?" I reached

for the bottle of hot sauce on the Lazy Susan in the middle of the table. "I think I'm maturing."

"Sure you are," he replied with a wink.

"Mmmm," I said as I shoveled a forkful of eggs into my mouth. After I'd chewed and swallowed. "Delicious."

Genevieve smiled. "Thank you kindly."

"Any chance there's coffee to be had?" Eddie asked.

"Oh God, yes," I gasped.

"That pot is almost always on." She gestured at an ancient-looking coffee pot in the corner by the sink.

I wanted to jump up and kiss her. Instead, I jumped up and ran for the coffee. Moments later, I was poured a scalding dose of caffeine down my throat while I set a second mug in front of Eddie.

"Ahhhh." I closed my eyes and let the caffeine fill my bloodstream. "I'm barely human without my coffee."

"You're barely human *with* coffee," Eddie retorted.

I kicked him under the table.

Genevieve laughed. "Sounds like Ty. He can't get going until he's had his morning sludge."

"Speaking of," Eddie said, "where is our fearless cowboy this morning?"

"Oh, he's always out the door before dawn," she replied, returning to the kitchen and setting the pan back on the stove. "But he's usually back in time for breakfast."

"Did someone say breakfast?"

The kitchen door swung open and Ty stepped inside. He wore pretty much the same uniform as yesterday, only his tee was green and his jeans a darker blue. He tugged the cap off his head and scrubbed a hand over his dark blond hair, lifting the hem of his shirt in the process and revealing a slice of his chiseled abs.

I shoved another bite of spicy egg into my mouth to hide the drool.

Focus, Cassie. Focus.

"Could someone grab the toast out of the oven?" Genevieve asked as she carried two more plates to the table.

Eddie the panther was to the oven and back with toast before she set the first plate down in front of Ty as he dropped into the seat at the head of the table. Genevieve took the chair next to mine.

The whole scene was entirely too domestic. As if we were four friends—or four family members—gathered together for a meal. The only thing that ruined the intimacy was the knowledge that Eddie's camera was filming our every move.

We ate quietly for several minutes until the silence got to me.

"We should get started as soon as possible," I said, shifting uncomfortably in my seat. "We need to maximize our shooting time. The more footage we get, the better. We want to give the editing team as much raw material as possible."

"I still can't quite believe the Black Willow is going to be on television." Genevieve grinned as she pushed eggs around on her plate. "It'll be great publicity."

"With the operation closed for an entire month," Ty said without looking up from his eggs, "it had better be.

"It will be," she insisted. "Besides, think of all the girls who will be beating down our door to meet the famous Ty Haywood."

Ty huffed out an awkward laugh. "I'll be happy if tourists

beat down our door to stay at the famous Black Willow Ranch."

"Oh shush," Genevieve continued, unfazed by her brother's reaction. "I've always wanted a famous big brother. And if it gets me one step closer to nieces and nephews then all the better."

I laughed. I couldn't help it.

I had barely known Genevieve for a day, and already I'd heard her lamenting her brother's single state several times. Given her determination, I was amazed he hadn't married just to get her off his back.

Ty shot me a sideways glance and then he started laughing too.

"She's persistent," I said.

He shook his head. "You have no idea."

"I can imagine."

"Just wait," he said. "She'll have you matched up with every eligible guy in Rocky Gulch before the week is out."

"I am still here, you know." She jabbed him in the shoulder.

Eddie got up from the table and went to grab his camera.

"Sometimes," Ty said, leaning in close to whisper, "I lock my door at night because I'm afraid she's going to sneak someone in."

"You do not!" she admonished.

"It's probably safer that way," I agreed. Then, when Genevieve smacked my arm, I added, "Or you might just be making her angry."

Genevieve pushed back from the table. "I give up."

"Aw, don't be mad." Ty grabbed her in a big bear hug from behind.

She threw an eye roll over her shoulder. "Whatever. You

three need to get out of my kitchen so I can clean up. Go—" She twisted out of Ty's hug and made a shooing gesture. "—do your Hollywood thing."

"Actually," I said, "it's a New York thing."

Genevieve ignored me.

Ty warned with a wink, "Be careful. You won't like her when she's angry."

I bit back a smile.

She threw a wet dishrag at her brother—who ducked so that the sopping cloth hit the wall behind him, knocking down a framed aerial photo of the ranch.

Ty reached down and picked it up.

"See what a good brother I am," he told me.

Genevieve turned on the water and squeezed dish soap into the sink, cheerfully returning to the task of cleaning up the breakfast dishes.

"Have a good day filming," she said. "Y'all try not to fall off the horse."

My heart thudded.

Right. Riding. I'd managed to put off the inevitable yesterday, but one of the first steps in cowgirl training was getting on a horse. There was no escaping it.

I had a sudden image of me with a broken neck, in traction and trapped in a Texas hospital indefinitely. Bud would fire me for sure.

"Fall off?" I echoed.

"I'll make sure your cinch is tight," Ty insisted. "I won't let you fall."

Every single cell in my body believed him.

With an angelic smile, Genevieve turned to him and said, "I was talking to you."

Then she blew him a kiss and he laughed again.

"I'll never understand that girl," he said and we headed out the kitchen door, Eddie right behind with the camera on his shoulder.

"You probably shouldn't try," I suggested. "She seems like a force."

Ty glanced at me as we crossed the back porch. "You have no idea."

I followed him down the steps. There were several other buildings around the house—some so small that they could only be for animals or equipment storage, others that were probably the bunkhouse where the ranch hands lived and the guests stayed.

"Come on," he said, leading us toward the barn. "We've got a cowgirl to make."

ROUGHSHOD LOOMED over me like Trump Tower, all tall and golden and utterly intimidating. She and I had been having a stare down while Ty adjusted her saddle, but now he called me around to the side.

"Put your foot in here," he said, pointing to something he called the stirrup.

My lesson had started with a detailed explanation of the horse-related gear—sorry, *tack*. I'd learned everything from the bit to the billet strap and everything in between. I was pretty certain I would forget it all by tomorrow. Or maybe even by that afternoon.

I looked at the distance between my foot and the stirrup.

"I don't think that's going to happen."

Ty grinned. "Of course it will."

I inched away a little.

"Trust me," he said. "You aren't the first greenhorn I've put in the saddle."

"Green what?"

"You're just going to pop up and sit for a minute." He waved me closer. "Get a feel for the girl."

Every city girl instinct inside me wanted to run—back to the house, back to the airport, *back to civilization*. But I caught a glimpse of Eddie from the corner of my eye and that reminded me why I was here. I was trying to salvage my career, and if that meant getting up on the back of a giant then that's what I was going to do.

"Just for a minute?" I echoed.

He nodded, his bright blue eyes sparkling.

The dimples should have warned me.

Putting one foot in front of the other, I walked to his side, lifted my foot and placed it in the stirrup. Okay, that wasn't as impossible as I'd imagined. But getting myself from the ground to the back of the horse was another matter. It seemed to defy the laws of physics.

"Now wha—"

Ty's hands wrapped around my waist and before I could blink he had lifted me up into the air. I stood there, hovering two feet off the ground, one foot stuck in the stirrup and my pelvis pressed into the side of the saddle.

"Swing your leg over her back."

"I—"

"Your other leg," he corrected when I tried to move the one that was resting in the stirrup.

Eyes closed, breath held, I forced my right leg over

Roughshod's back. As I dropped into the seat of the saddle, a leg dangling from either side of the horse, Ty released me.

"Don't let go!" I shouted.

"Relax," he said, resting one hand on my thigh and the other on Roughshod's neck. "I've got you."

That should have been reassuring, but Roughshod chose that moment to shift her weight. I grabbed the saddle horn with both hands.

"Don't squeeze your legs," he said, as I was about to do just that. "It'd signal her to speed up. Relax your mind and your body, and that will relax the horse."

Relax? Was he insane? I was sitting *on top of a horse*! There was nothing relaxing about that. The rocking lull of the subway, that was relaxing. A full body massage was relaxing. Compared to this, even New Year's Eve in Times Square was relaxing.

I was the opposite of relaxed. My heart stuttered and I wished I hadn't left my field kit back in the tack room. I definitely needed a Xanax.

Babe, who had found us in the barn after her morning romp through the pasture, stood with her paws on the top rail of the fence. Watching. Like I was the best entertainment ever.

If she barked, this was all over.

My eyes were probably wild as I looked at Eddie, silently begging him to get me out of there. He remained passively professional behind the lens.

"There's my good girl," Ty whispered to the horse, rubbing his hand over her neck. "You're a gentle one."

Even though he was talking to the horse, his hand didn't move from my thigh. It was like he and Roughshod were alone in the arena. Ty murmured in her ear, she nickered in his.

The more the two of them ignored me, the more… comfortable I became. Not quite at ease, but slightly less terrified. I felt my muscles began to unclench and I could feel my breathing deepen.

"Now, I'm going to lead you in a bit of a walk—"

"Walk?" I squawked. "You said I was just going to sit up here."

He turned his glittering eyes up at me. "I lied."

Those dimples.

I watched, in horror, as he grabbed the lead line attached to Roughshod's halter and started walking. I held the saddle horn in a death grip while trying to force my legs to stay relaxed. Crying might have made for a good TV moment, but I was determined not to let this situation break me.

The horse took one step and my weight shifted to the left. Before I could scream, she took another and I shifted back the other way. As she moved forward I gradually got used to shifting my weight back and forth to keep centered in the saddle.

By the time Ty walked us around the entire pen and back to the starting point I was feeling like an old pro.

"That wasn't so hard?" he asked as he helped me down to the ground. "Now was it?"

"No, it—"

My breath caught as I slid down the side of the horse and found myself sandwiched between her body and Ty's tee-covered chest. Once I had my feet on the ground, to twisted around to face him. I sucked in a deep breath and inhaled the scent of hay and horse and something undefinably male.

Don't look up, I warned myself. *Don't look into his—*

Too late.

I lifted my head and met his blue eyes straight on. From this close I could see the tiny lines around his eyes when he smiled and how his lashes curled up in an enviable way.

"Is the, um—" I swallowed and tried to regain some of my composure. "Is that the end of the lesson."

He tilted his head slightly to the side. "Not quite. You've got to learn how to put a horse away properly."

"H-how do I do that?"

"I thought you'd never ask."

When he moved away, my body wanted to follow. But just then Eddie moved into a new position and I jerked myself back into reality. This wasn't *real* reality. It was reality TV. I wasn't at the Black Willow to swoon over some hot cowboy, to have some kind of fling that could never work beyond the term of my sentence in the Texas outback. I was here to film a show, resurrect my career, and get back to New York as quickly as possible. With no dangling strings left behind.

I was, above all else, a professional. I could keep these feelings from complicating an already difficult situation.

We walked Roughshod to the barn, took off her tack, and brushed her down before sending her back into the pasture with her friends. She bounded across the field like a child at recess. A moment of pure joy.

At my side, Eddie was filming me. I gestured at him to turn his lens on the horses, but he leaned out from behind the camera to give me a dubious look.

Right. The horses weren't the story. *I* was the story. That was a hard thing to keep in mind.

Still, we needed setting and environmental footage. I nodded, smiling as he turned his camera to capture the equine reunion.

Ty was just locking the gate when a phone started ringing.

He jogged into the barn and grabbed a bright red, corded —*corded!*—phone off the wall.

"Yeah?" he answered. He stood tense as he listened. "Aw, hell, not again." He grabbed his ball cap and roughed a hand over his head. "No, we're finished up here. I'll take care of it."

As he hung up the phone, he turned to face me.

"Our fence line's been compromised," he said, walking toward a rusty shed across the drive. "Some of our cattle got onto McLaren property."

I didn't know how to respond, so I silently followed him to the shed. Eddie fell in step beside me. Ty pulled open the door, stepped inside, and emerged a moment later carrying a toolbox and a spool of wire.

He walked around the side of the shed, to a vehicle that looked like a golf cart on steroids. The thing was bright green with yellow seats, had four seats, off-road tires, and a heavy-duty roll bar.

"What are you going to do?" I asked, watching as he set his armload on the cargo platform that jutted out the back.

"Me?" He turned back to me, smiling. "I think you mean *we*, city girl. This is part of cowgirl life. *We* are going to go herd the cattle back onto our property and repair the fence."

My heart thudded a little at the way he said *we*.

When I had climbed into the passenger seat and Eddie had positioned himself in the center of the back, Ty started down the road at teeth-rattling speed. I had a feeling this operation wouldn't be as simple as he'd made it sound.

FIVE

"WELL, DON'T YOU THREE LOOK..." Genevieve looked up from the computer in the corner of the kitchen as we tromped through the door. "...colorful."

I was so exhausted I could barely lift my feet. Babe nudged past me to race inside and nearly knocked me over.

I might have said something that came out sounding like, "Gahungh."

"Don't even start, Gen," Ty said as he set his Yankees cap—the only part of his wardrobe that wasn't caked in mud—on the counter. "That Buttercup is a slippery girl."

He tried to sound irritated, but a smile still hovered at the corners of his mouth. Ty was never far from a smile.

"Again?" Genevieve asked. "That's three days in a row."

Eddie, whose mud didn't rise above knee level because he'd insisted on keeping the camera clean—I'd insisted he was a wuss, but he hadn't risen to the bait—set the precious camera down next to Ty's cap. "But she makes for good television."

I could only imagine. The footage of me, diving headfirst

after a cow and winding up slip-sliding through a mud puddle —that was Emmy-winning material.

For the third time in three days, the small herd of cattle on the Black Willow had broken through the fence line that bordered the McLaren ranch to the south. For the third time, Ty and I—with the help of the Black Willow's two resident ranch hands—had to chase the cattle back onto Haywood land and then repair the fence.

Watching Ty was a thing of pure masculine beauty. Back muscles straining against his tee, gloved hands unrolling and twisting the fencing wire, teasing the cows as he shooed them back onto his land. It was clear that he reveled in the challenge of hard work.

I reveled in watching him, but the exhaustion was starting to outweigh the appeal. If the cattle escaped again, I might petition for their permanent freedom.

This time Ty had triple-reinforced the wire.

Eddie set his camera down on the counter and called for Babe. It was a testament to his lack of exhaustion that when Babe stood and placed her paws on his chest, he did not so much as stumble.

I glared at him and grumbled something unintelligible.

"Are you okay, Cassie?" Genevieve asked.

I focused my energy on forming words. "Tired. So very tired." I was hungry, too, but the tired part definitely won out. "I think I'll just head to bed early."

So what if the sun hadn't even set yet. After three full days as a cowgirl I had earned some slack. Three days already felt like a lifetime. How was I ever going to last a month?

"Why don't you take a bath?" Genevieve suggested.

"There's a huge claw-foot in the master bath. That always soaks my day away."

"That"—*oh my sweet bubble bath*—"sounds amazing."

"Come on," she said, getting up from the computer and heading for the stairs. "I'll show you where everything is."

As I followed Genevieve up to the second floor, my legs muscles cried every step of the way. Leg muscle I was pretty sure hadn't existed before this week. No yoga or spin class had ever found them, but apparently cowgirling was a more thorough form of exercise.

"Ranch work is harder than I thought," I said as we reached the top. "My city girl body wasn't prepared."

"It's a hard life," she agreed. "But it's the only one I've ever known. I'm sure I wouldn't make it two minutes in the big city." She pushed open the door at the end of the hall. "The miracle tub is in here."

When Genevieve suggested the bath, I had assumed the room was hers. But as I took in the plain blue bedding, the tees and jeans draped over nearly every surface, and the smell of leather and something spicy in the air, I knew this was a man's bedroom.

I knew it was Ty's bedroom.

"Don't look at the mess," she complained as we crossed the room. "I've given up trying to keep it clean. I make him shut the door so I don't have to see it."

I hurried through. It felt too much like an invasion to be in his space.

"I have to hide the bubble bath." Genevieve opened the cabinet under the sink and reached into the back before pulling out a bottle of lime green liquid.

"He doesn't like seeing it?" I asked.

"No," she said, handing me the bottle. "He likes *using* it. This stuff is too expensive to waste as body wash."

I laughed, taking the bottle of bubble bath from her. "Thanks. I won't use too much."

"Use as much as you like. It's nice having a girl around and besides…" She gave me a look halfway between a smile and a frown. "You look like you could use it."

I didn't have to glance down at my mud-covered body to know that I looked like a disaster area. My nose had gotten used to it, but I probably smelled just as lovely.

"Thanks," I said as Genevieve started to leave.

At the door, she turned back. "Tomorrow, you should borrow some of my work clothes."

"No, that's all right." At that moment, I dropped my head and got a good look at the state of my clothes. No one looking at me then could have known I was wearing black jeans, a black t-shirt, and very expensive black shoes. "But access to a washing machine would be great."

"Downstairs, at the end of the hall." Genevieve smiled. "And I'll leave a set of work clothes on your bed. Just in case."

She left, closing the bathroom behind her. A second later I heard the bedroom door close too. I was alone in the bathroom and the beautiful porcelain tub was calling to me.

Five minutes later, I was soaking away the aches and the mud in a steaming hot bath, inhaling the scent of lime and coconut, and pretending I was miles away on a tropical beach. Not that I'd ever been on a tropical beach, but I had seen pictures. My mind drifted, picturing white sands and blue waters, hearing the wash of the waves on the shore, smelling the salty sea, swimming after mermaids… or hunky mermen with blue eyes and dark blond hair…

The pounding woke me.

I lurched up in the tub and my heart raced in my chest.

More pounding. Well, knocking actually.

"Cassie, you in there?" Ty asked through the door.

"Yeah, I—" My hands went instinctively over my chest, even though the door was still closed, all too aware of what I wasn't wearing beneath the layer of foamy bubbles. "Is something wrong?"

"Sorry to intrude," he said. "Gen's out collecting from the chickens."

"What?"

"I mean, I wouldn't normally—" He stopped and started again. "Gen should be the one to—" Another hesitation. "You have a call on the house phone."

"Oh," I said. "Okay. Thanks. I'll be right down."

It had to be Bud, calling to check up on me. No one else had the Haywoods' number.

Twisting myself up, I pulled the rubber plug from the tub drain and then grabbed the light blue towel I had set on the stool next to the bath. As the coconut lime bathwater swirled down the drain, I quickly dried off and wrapped the towel around my chest.

When I first followed Genevieve into the bathroom, I hadn't planned on going back downstairs. I hadn't thought to have clothes waiting—I had been single-mindedly focused on sinking into a day-erasing bath. And, I realized as I crossed to the door, the magic bath had worked. My leg muscles weren't nearly as angry anymore.

Now all I had to do was to sneak down the hall to my room and pull on my pajamas before—

"Aaack!"

My feet slipped out from under me as I reached for the door handle. Instinct took over, and somehow I managed to stay upright *and* keep my towel in place.

"Cassie?" Ty threw open the door. "Are you okay?"

"Yeah, I—" I made a fluttering gesture with my free hand. "I slipped on the wet tile is all. I'm fine."

"You're sure?" he asked, as if not quite trusting my insistence. His bright blue eyes scanned over my thankfully-still-towel-covered body.

Every inch of my skin tingled.

"Positive," I breathed.

"Here," he said, stepping forward and wrapping a strong, warm hand around my upper arm, "let me help."

He guided me onto the dry wood floor of the bedroom.

No one would ever accuse me of being a girly girl—but in that moment, standing in Ty's bedroom with his hand on my arm and nothing but a towel to cover me, I had the most ridiculous urge to giggle.

"Thanks," I said, stepping away before I did something stupid. "I'd better go…"

"Yeah, your phone call."

I nodded and then headed for the door.

"Hey Cassie," he said. When I looked back at him, he added, "Be careful."

Good advice.

Be careful, Cassie. That way lies trouble and complication.

But moments later, as I hurried downstairs to take my phone call, I totally giggled. That advice might have come too late. Trouble had already arrived.

"MR. GORMAN," I said as I held the phone up to my ear. "Sorry you had to wait."

He didn't answer right away. Instead, I heard a muffled, "No, I don't want hot chocolate, Anne. I want scotch. Two fingers."

I couldn't hear his wife Anne's response.

I exchanged an eye roll with Eddie, who had my laptop open and was reviewing the day's footage. After training day one, I'd been too exhausted to cut the dailies for Bud, so Eddie took over the task. The two he'd done so far had been terrific. If today's clip looked just as good I would tell him to start sending them without waiting for my approval.

"Just get me the damn drink," Bud grumbled in my ear. Then, "Bishop, you there yet?"

"Yes, Mr. Gorman," I answered. "Sorry about the wait."

I heard the clink of ice against glass.

"Thank you," he said, not to me. "Now, what is this crap you gave me?"

I stayed silent, assuming he was still talking to Anne.

"Bishop!" he barked. "Are you listening?"

Eddie glanced at me.

"Yes sir." Great. *Not* talking to Anne. I dropped my head into my left hand and squeezed at my temples with the thumb and middle finger. "I'm sorry, did you mean the clips are crap?"

My foot brushed against something big a furry. Babe didn't move as I set my feet on her side. She made a comfy footstool.

"Of course they are." Bud took a loud gulp of his scotch. "What the hell is going on there?"

Maybe this wasn't about the daily clips. He hadn't

responded to my email from three days ago, explaining that the princess hadn't shown up. Maybe he never read it.

"I should have called, sir," I explained. "The bi—" I stopped myself, remembering that the sun-bathing princess was some relation of his. "The young woman who was supposed to play the cowgirl couldn't make it, sir. I made an in-the-moment decision to step in myself. To keep the production on track."

"I know that," he boomed. "I read your damned email. And stop with this sir crap. I mean the content is garbage."

"I'm sorry, s—" I squeezed my temples harder. Maybe if I pinched hard enough I would pass out and be spared the rest of this conversation. "What can I do?"

"You can stop acting like you're afraid of the dang camera. Start acting like you really want to learn how to be a cowgirl." He huffed out a low sigh. "This show is supposed to be about people getting to live out their fantasies. Not being forced into some kind of torture experiment. Start acting like your career depends on you *wanting* to ride the damn horse."

"Yes, s—" I released my temples. "Okay, I can do that."

"You're only going through the motions." A heavy thunk of glass on wood echoed through the phone. "I know you didn't want the role, but it's one of the smartest decisions you've made lately."

"It is?"

The praise, the first I'd had in a long time, was a welcome sound. I sat up straighter.

Under the table, Babe turned around so her head was resting on my feet.

"You're about as far from a cowgirl as anyone I've ever seen," But continued. "It'll play great in the teasers. *The TV producer with cowgirl dreams.* Soccer moms will eat that crap up. But you've got to make us believe that you want to try. Make us believe it's your lifelong dream. Otherwise the audience isn't rooting for you. Got it?"

"Yes, s—" I switched the phone to my other hand. "Yes, I got it."

"Good, because Bishop?"

"Yes?"

"If the next clips don't cut it, I'm pulling the plug."

I nodded even though he couldn't see me. When the line went dead in my ear, I set my phone down and let my forehead fall to the table. Babe started licking my freshly-bathed toes.

Bud was right. The show's hook was fantasy fulfillment. If it didn't look like I was fulfilling my fantasy, then the whole thing would look fake. It would look like the setup that it actually.

That was the double-edged sword of reality television. Everything had to both look like spontaneous action while providing some kind of coherent storyline. Sometimes situations had to be manipulated, reshot, or even completely overhauled in order to fit the narrative. Fake had to look real. Even a hint of fabrication would send audiences running for their remotes.

"Bad news?" Ty asked.

I jerked upright. "What? No," I insisted. "Just... No, it's fine."

Eddie handed me my purse and I flashed him a grateful smile. I popped a pair of antacid chews into my mouth. The chalky texture was at the same time disgusting and reassuring.

It was fine. Because I *had* been going through the motions. I had been doing everything with a grimace and a silent wish that I was back in the city, with nothing more strenuous in my day than lugging a package back to my apartment—and even then, if the package was too heavy, I'd take a cab. No, if I was going to make this show work, I had to want this cowgirl dream.

At the very least, I had to look like I wanted it.

"Chuck that montage," I told Eddie. "We're starting fresh tomorrow."

We wouldn't delete the footage, because there had to be a lot of good raw material, but there was no point in sending Bud more of the same.

"You're sure?" Eddie asked.

I nodded.

Babe moved her licking attentions up to my ankles.

I pushed away from the table. There was no way I was letting Bud pull the plug on *Try It On*. I'd already endured three days of serious cowgirl work, and I wasn't about to let my aching muscles and screaming joints be in vain. I would make this production work if it killed me.

When my stomach lurched at the thought, I popped another antacid.

SIX

AFTER A NIGHT of restless dreams that involved neon cattle and Wizard of Oz-worthy dust storms, I finally jerked awake when a massive video camera started chasing me through the barn. Deep-seeded psychological worries much?

Heart pounding, I bolted up in bed and was shocked to find the room still in virtual darkness. The distant howl of the screaming dog, which Ty had explained was actually a coyote, told me why I was awake when my alarm hadn't gone off. A faint amber glow filtered in through the lace curtains.

It felt like I had been sleeping for days.

I groped for my phone—aka the useless piece of technology now relegated to digital notepad and alarm clock—and saw that it was barely six. With a groan, I fell back onto the bed.

Sure, this was the latest I'd snoozed in the almost-week I'd been in Texas, but I had definitely earned a sleep-in today. Especially after last night's phone call.

Bud's words throbbed in my mind.

Make us believe that you want to try.

Make us believe it's your lifelong dream.

I grabbed the bottle of antacids.

My mind played back through the comp clips Bud showed me when he gave me the assignment. The spouse swapping. The unskilled DIYers. The home-body world travelers. As I rolled tape in my mind, one recurring theme played out, over and over. In each and every scenario, the uprooted ordinary, the person completely out of their element in the crazy situation, was trying. Really, truly, fully *trying*.

They were giving it their all to try to adapt to and overcome the extraordinary circumstances. And I knew, if I was being completely honest with myself, I was not.

Sure, I'd tried riding the horse and I'd attempted the roping and the mucking and the grooming. But Bud was right, I'd only been going through the motions. I didn't really want to know how to groom a horse, so why bother actually learning.

The entire premise of the show was to watch someone get to live out a fantasy or, at the very least, to experience a completely different way of life. I was only trying to make good television.

I closed my eyes and draped my forearm over my face to block out the encroaching dawn.

I hadn't been really trying, and clearly that had shown on the tape.

If I'd learned anything in my years in film and television it was that you can't hide anything from the camera. I might have thought I was doing my best, giving it my best shot. But the camera saw through the facade. The camera saw, and then it told everyone who watched the replay.

As much as I wanted to argue and insist that everything was fine, that the audience would love it when they saw the final cut… I knew that audiences didn't lie. If they weren't getting it, they weren't getting it. No amount of pouting or arguing or denial could change that.

Besides, at this point Bud was the only audience I needed to impress and he was anything but.

"I *don't* want to do this," I complained to the empty room. "I didn't sign up to play cowgirl."

Even as I said the words, I knew how very whiny they sounded. I rarely indulged in self-pity, but if any situation warranted it then I was pretty sure this one did.

Still, it wouldn't do me any good. Feeling sorry for myself wouldn't bring the missing princess to heel and wouldn't make the tape look any better.

I drew in a deep breath through my nose and let it out through my mouth. I couldn't remember if that's what the yoga instructor Bethany once dragged me to had suggested, but it did help calm the rising tide of panic. That, and a couple more antacid chews.

This was so not my fault. If the jet-setting Hollywood princess had just shown up, we would all be sitting back, laughing at her awkward attempts to ride a horse and rope a cow.

But there was no point in crying over spoiled trust fund divas. I'd stepped into the role, and now there was no going back.

How on earth was I going to make both Bud and the audience believe that living the cowgirl lifestyle was my ultimate fantasy? Especially when my real fantasy involved being sandwiched between Spielberg and Scorsese at an awards show. I'd never wanted to live anywhere but New York. I'd never wanted to be anything but a filmmaker.

No, that wasn't exactly true. Back in high school I wanted to be a fashion designer. Only my mother's insistence that I receive a proper education had sent me to Columbia instead of FIT. But becoming a glamorous, world-renowned fashion designer was a far cry from the dust-covered cowgirl life.

I gave myself a few more seconds to wallow in my whiny attitude. A few seconds, and then I would pack it away until I was out of this no-win situation.

When I had whined enough that I was starting to annoy myself, I swung my legs out of the bed and pushed to my feet. I had to find my zen. Find my—in actor-speak—inner motivation. I had to find that thing inside of me that connected with the cowgirl dream.

Thinking back to my fashion design dream, I tried to pinpoint what had been so very appealing. Fashion itself had never held much appeal for me—as my closet full of all-black basics and Bethany's eternal dismay were living testament. Why then had I thought designing clothes would be so great?

As I pictured some of the outfits I'd designed in the back of Algebra II class, I realized they all had an element of fantasy, an element of costume. More than just clothes, I'd been creating characters. The clothes had just been a shortcut.

Maybe clothes were the key. Maybe if I embraced the cowgirl costume, I would feel closer to being a real cowgirl. I would feel closer to the dream of becoming one.

It couldn't hurt to try.

I crossed to the corner of the room where my suitcase had burst open on the floor. I pulled the black tank top I was wearing off over my head and threw it onto the massive pile of black clothes I'd brought. I only had a black bra, but that was going to have to do.

As I clasped the cotton tab behind my back, I moved to the chest of drawers where I had stashed the stack of clothes Genevieve set out for me the other night. I pulled out a pair of dark wash jeans—*baby steps, Cassie, baby steps*—a soft gray tee, and a blue and gray plaid western shirt with short sleeves and a pair of chest pockets.

I stared at the clothes. Bethany would hardly call them colorful—to the woman who regularly worn brightly hued sundresses, I was sure the blue and gray were downright drab —but this was the most color I had worn since I stopped letting Mom put me in corduroy jumpers in sixth grade. My wardrobe had been nothing but black since middle school.

"Desperate times," I whispered.

I stepped into the jeans, amazed to find they actually fit. They might have been only slightly more blue than my normal jeans, but they were a thousand times softer and at least ten times more curve-hugging. *This,* I thought as I yanked up the zipper, *is what jeans should feel like.*

The gray tee followed quickly—thankfully the fabric was thick enough to hide the black bra beneath—and then the western shirt. When I stepped into view of the small mirror sitting on the chest of drawers, I was prepared to not recognize the woman reflected back at me. To my surprise, she looked just like me. Only her cheeks looked a little brighter and her eyes a little bluer.

The color somehow managed to make me look fresher, younger maybe.

This was what Bethany had always been trying to tell me, but I'd never been willing to listen. I'd never even given color a chance. But now that I had…

"I will never hear the end of this," I told my reflection.

I couldn't hide the evidence—this was intended to be broadcast on national television after all—but if Bethany knew that I actually liked how the color looked, she would be forever shoving brighter and brighter clothes my direction.

My reflection eyed me warily. "This will be our little secret," I told her, biting back a smile. "Bethan can never know."

We nodded at each other and then I sank down onto the end of the bed. I reached down and grabbed the pair of boots —honest-to-goodness cowboy boots—that Genevieve had given me. They were a golden, honey color, with a soft sueded finish and a short stacked heel. I rolled on a pair of socks—black, because I couldn't just abandon all my years of embracing the dark—and then slid my right foot into the right boot. A moment later, the left foot followed, and suddenly I was no longer Cassie Bishop, die-hard city chick. I was Cassie Bishop, cowgirl in training.

I could do this.

SEVEN

THE NEXT COUPLE days passed in a blur of learning to ride Roughshod, doing ranch-related chores, and generally working myself into exhaustion—while Eddie filmed every last dusty detail. My mother, who always insisted on a cook, a car service, and a housekeeper, would be appalled. Personally, I was too exhausted to be anything but grateful when I walked into the kitchen Thursday morning and Genevieve said that Ty had gone into town, that I had the morning off from cowgirl duty. My muscles did a victory dance.

"I'm not afraid of hard work," I insisted as I followed Genevieve out to her beloved chicken coop an hour later. "I'm just…"

"Not used to it," she filled in. "I know."

"Horses and cows are scarce in the New York metro area." I tightened my palm around the woven basket that was supposed to carry the eggs. "The co-op in my neighborhood has chickens, but I've never had time to get involved."

Or the inclination, really. I was content getting my eggs at the local market and never seeing the face my food originally came with. Bonding with cows and chickens felt like a bit of a betrayal if I was still going to eat hamburgers and nuggets.

"Don't worry, you're doing great," Genevieve insisted.

Eddie snorted. I gave him an over-bright smile.

Genevieve hauled open the door to the chicken coop and waved me inside.

I sucked in a breath—and immediately regretted it. Not the freshest smelling place I'd ever been. The audience should be thankful smell-o-vision had never taken off as an idea. There was enough dust in the air to mark the streaks of sunlight slanting in through the cracks in the wooden walls. It would be a great setting shot.

A quick glance over my shoulder told me Eddie was already filming it. Exactly why he was my go-to guy.

"There's always a period of adjustment. You should have seen Ty when he first got back," Genevieve said, stepping in after me. "You'd have thought he never rode a horse in his life."

"Got back?" I asked.

"He didn't tell you?" She smiled, like she was both confused and amused. "Ty went to school in New York."

"New York?" I sucked in so much chicken smell and dust-filled air I erupted into a coughing fit. "Like, *New York*, New York?"

Genevieve nodded.

Ty Haywood, the ultimate Texas cowboy—with his rough hands, dirty boots, and knee-melting drawl—had lived in a city? In *my* city? It was almost too much to believe.

"No way," I stammered.

"Sure did." She walked up to a shelf of straw-filled nests

and reached into the first one. "College and graduate school. Worked a couple years at some big engineering firm until..."

Her voice trailed off. From the slight catch in tone, I had a feeling I knew what she was going to say.

"Your parents?" I asked quietly.

I knew from the dossier that Ty and Genevieve's parents had died in a late-night car crash a few years ago. The casting director had even included a printout of a news article from a local paper. *Rancher and wife dead after head-on collision with tractor-trailer.*

According to the article, they had been on their way home after dropping Ty off at the airport. Genevieve had decided to stay home rather than make the trip into the city with them.

I hadn't asked either of them about it because it seemed wrong that I knew something so personal without knowing them all that well and because it wasn't the kind of thing that belonged on a show like this. Maybe if I were filming a documentary about the realities of life on a modern ranch. But not for *Try It On.*

Genevieve nodded sadly. "They were so happy when he got the scholarship. That he would have a chance to have a life outside of Rocky Gulch..."

She shook her head, as if the memory was too much to talk about. Too personal. Too raw.

This was not for public viewing.

I quickly exchanged a look with Eddie, nodding toward the door. We were here to shoot hi-jinx and hard work—some sexual tension between me and the aforementioned cowboy or some embarrassing moments of me falling off a horse. Not emotional confessions.

Eddie understood.

"I'm going to step outside," he said, maneuvering his way through the small door. "Need a few exterior shots of the coop."

"Good idea," I said.

Genevieve slipped her hand into my basket and set a small brown egg inside.

"He came home when they died," she said as soon as Eddie was gone, and almost so quietly I didn't hear. "He had a promising career and a life in the city, and he gave it all up to come back and help me."

This fit the picture of Ty I had come to know in the last few days. It was obvious he worried about his little sister and that he put a high priority on family and duty. What other choice could he have made?

"I was raised to ranching too," she continued. "When I was young, I had other dreams, but with Ty gone and my fiancé eager to take over the day-to-day operations when Daddy retired, the future of the Black Willow fell to me. Aaron had called off the wedding about six months before the accident. I was afraid I couldn't run the Black Willow on my own. We would have had to sell."

She wiped at her eyes.

"I feel so guilty," she confessed. "He gave up everything because of me."

"I'm sure he doesn't feel that way."

I didn't know Ty any better than I did Genevieve, but he didn't seem like the kind of guy who would want someone feeling guilty over that. Or like the kind of guy who would let someone talk him into doing something he didn't want to do. If Ty came home after the accident, I had a feeling it was because he *wanted* to come home.

"He wouldn't say it." She gave me a watery smile. "But that doesn't change the truth."

"Maybe you should talk to him about this."

I had no idea why she felt so comfortable sharing with me. Then again, it wasn't like there were any other women on the ranch to listen. Only a couple of ranch hands who looked like they would be uncomfortable with the mere mention of the word *feelings*.

Either way, telling Ty how she felt could only make things better.

"He keeps everything wrapped up so tight." She huffed out a tight breath. "I always feel like I make him worse while he's trying so hard to make things better."

In her sad smile I saw the same pain I'd felt when my dad passed.

"And some things can't get better," I replied.

Before I knew what I was doing, I stepped forward and wrapped her in a tight hug. I wasn't usually the comforting, maternal type, but I understood what she was feeling—what she was going through. And I knew that nothing would make it better.

She hugged me back and I felt the kind of bond I imagined between sisters.

"Thank you," she whispered. "For listening."

For several long moments, we just stood there—amidst the chicken smell and the dusty air.

A soft cough from the doorway warned me that Eddie was ready to get back to work.

"It's safe," Genevieve called out before I could. "The crying's over."

I should have known she saw my subtle nudge to get Eddie

to leave us alone for a minute. She was a smart girl. And, apparently, her brother was a smart guy.

"So tell me everything about Ty in New York," I said as I joined her at the nesting boxes. "This is something I definitely need to know."

By the time we returned to the house, we had more than a dozen eggs and I knew a lot more about a certain handsome cowboy and the many layers beneath his Yankees cap. And I was intrigued to find out even more.

A COUPLE HOURS LATER, Genevieve and I had gathered the eggs, changed the linens on all the beds, cleaned and put away the breakfast dishes, and started a pot of beans soaking for dinner.

So much for my morning off. Apparently the work was never done around the ranch—or the ranch house.

"That certainly goes faster with an extra pair of hands," she said, dusting her hands on her apron before reaching behind her to untie the strings.

"What's next?" I asked.

Even though I'd been exhausted when I hauled my lazy butt down the stairs a few short hours ago, now I felt energized. It seemed counterintuitive, but working had made me *less* tired.

Genevieve laughed at my enthusiasm, but before she could answer the sound of boot steps in the hall echoed into the room.

"Are you stealing my cowhand?" Ty asked, forearms braced on either side of the doorway and leaning into the room.

My eyes widened at the sight of him and my breath caught a little. He had shaved, his chiseled features no longer softened by a layer of soft stubble, and he was wearing a button-down shirt instead of the t-shirts he normally wore. He had even traded his dirty work boots for classic cowboy boots with pointed toes and shiny leather. Whatever business took him to town must have been professional business.

My jaw hung slack at his makeover. I found myself imagining what he would look like all the way dressed up. The aura of cowboy was too heavy, though. I couldn't quite picture him in a full tuxedo, climbing the steps at Lincoln Center.

I had a feeling that his current look was more appealing than a penguin suit could ever be. There was a lot to be said for a pair of perfectly worn jeans and a soft tee, too.

"I was only keeping her busy," Genevieve said, her voice full of laughter. "I'm sure she'd rather be doing hard labor than helping me clean house."

I choked a little. "Well, I wouldn't say *that*…"

Ty turned his attention to me, and I swore I could feel the burn of his gaze. "Come on, city gal," he said with a lazy smile. "Let's get you back to work."

Eddie snickered as I stifled a groan. Sure, *he* wasn't the one going through the daily cowgirl triathlon. All he had to do was keep up well enough to film it.

I twisted back to stick my tongue out. The editor could cut that out later.

"I need to change out of these dress duds," Ty said. "I'll meet you on the back porch in five."

As I opened the back door, Genevieve called out, "Thank you for the help this morning."

I leaned back into the kitchen. "Any time."

And I was surprised by how much I meant it.

Less than two minutes later, Ty walked out the back door looking more like his normal self. Except for the close shave. I couldn't help but steal a glance at just how well those well-worn jeans fit his backside as he crossed the porch.

"Today," he said, sauntering down the steps and onto the lawn, "you're going to learn how to muck a stall."

"Great," I replied.

He threw me a wry look that I didn't understand until we arrived at the barn a few minutes later and he explained what mucking meant. It was *not* as fun as it sounded.

He handed me a pitchfork and, after a brief instruction, pointed me to a dirty stall. He started shoveling out the next stall over.

After making an exaggerated gagging sound, Eddie chose a position on the opposite side of the aisle and settled in to film from a distance.

"So," I said as I hauled a scoop of manure out into the wheelbarrow in the aisle, "New York, huh?"

If I was going to spend the afternoon cleaning out horse stalls, he was going to answer some burning questions.

He joined me at the wheelbarrow. "How did you—?"

I raised my eyebrows.

"Genevieve," Ty said with fake anger in his tone, but I could hear the smile. "I should have known that wouldn't stay secret for long."

"If that's the best of your secrets, you've led a pretty boring life."

He winked at me, then turned back to the stall.

I returned to mine and repeated my question.

"Yes ma'am," he answered. "I was a bona fide New Yorker. For almost eight years."

Eight years? Between college, grad school, and work I guessed that made sense. But still. That was a long time to be away from the ranch. No wonder he had been a little rusty when he got back.

I asked, "Where did you live?"

"Hamilton Heights when I was in college," he said. "Then I commuted from Hoboken for graduate school and work."

"Hoboken?" I laughed. "I'm not sure I can be seen talking to a Jersey guy."

Ty shrugged. "I liked the small town feel." He finished his stall and stepped into mine. "Reminded me of home."

I could see that. With its quiet streets and community focus, Hoboken sometimes felt like a world away from New York. There were neighborhoods in Brooklyn with the same feel. But I loved being in the middle of everything in Manhattan. Anywhere else I would have felt isolated.

"If you're going to live in Jersey," I said as we worked side-by-side, "then I guess Hoboken is a decent choice."

"The home of Frank Sinatra can't be all bad," Ty teased.

"Frank is a classic."

We finished up my stall and moved on to the next. Apparently Ty had decided I worked too slowly, so we tackled the rest of the stalls together.

Exhaustion hit me halfway through the barn and I had to take a break. Leaning on my pitchfork, I asked, "Hamilton Heights? Does that mean you were at City College?"

He kept mucking. "They have a decent engineering program."

"Let me guess," I said, trying not to overtly ogle his

rippling back muscles as he stabbed and lifted the manure and dirty straw—not only was the environment pretty gross, but there was a camera and an eagle-eyed cameraman watching my every move. "Mechanical?"

Ty glanced at me over his shoulder. "Civil, actually. I wanted to design bridges and railroads."

There was something in his tone that made me ask, "But...?"

"But," he said as he hefted a load onto his pitchfork, "I ended up designing sewer systems for luxury resort properties."

I grimaced. "Yay...."

"I didn't hate it." He stabbed his pitchfork straight down and joined me on my break. "It just wasn't what I really wanted to be doing."

Eddie decided to brave the stench of the wheelbarrow and moved closer.

"Bridges and railroads," I suggested.

Ty shook his head. "Riding and ranching."

I smiled. Not only because I'd been right when I told Genevieve that Ty must have wanted to come home, but also because I could practically feel his joy. The subtle crinkle in the corners of his eyes, the faint echo of dimples. He loved every last second of his time on the ranch. Even mucking stalls.

"You would never go back?"

"Living in the city was like being in the eye of a twister," he said. "I couldn't see the chaos until I stepped outside of it."

That summed up city life perfectly. It was the thing I loved most about it, the frenetic energy. Constant motion, constant activity.

I looked around at the quiet barn. Eddie's camera was the

only thing modern within sight. "Pretty much the opposite of everything here."

"Not always." Ty stepped closer and lifted his hand. "Every so often we get a shock of chaos, right here in Rocky Gulch."

I watched, transfixed, as his fingers moved closer and closer. I felt the featherlight touch against my temple, and then it was gone. He held up a piece of straw for my inspection.

"In the city it's too easy to miss them," he said with a slow smile. "Out here, the contrast makes them stand out—makes them easier to appreciate."

My heart pitter-pattered. Honest-to-goodness pitter-pattered. Had Ty heard it? From the glint in his eye, I assumed he had.

Movement in my peripheral vision snapped me out of the moment.

Ty turned away as Eddie reminded us of his presence. Whatever just passed between me and the cowboy, that wasn't meant for television. But the camera never slept. The camera didn't miss a moment of my life out here.

I would do well to remember that.

Yanking my pitchfork out of the ground, I followed Ty into the next stall and started mucking. Still, no matter how much I tried to think about the ever-present camera, the inevitability of my return to New York, and the disgusting circumstances of our current work, I couldn't keep the smile off my face.

EIGHT

"DON'T LIE TO ME." My breakfast spoon dropped from my hand, hitting the table with an excited clatter. "Seriously?"

Ty nodded in that casual way he had, but I could see the tiniest hint of a smile tugging at his lips.

"We're going into the city?" I echoed. "Into the city. Like, *into* the city?"

The moment Ty uttered the words, *We're going into the city,* my blood pressure skyrocketed.

"I have some business," he explained. "We're not even staying the night."

I exchanged an ecstatic look with Eddie—or, with Eddie's camera—as I thought of all the possibilities. After being trapped in the middle of nowhere for more than a week, the thought of even a few hours in actual civilization sent goosebumps over my skin.

Saturday in the city sounded like the perfect medicine for my country fever.

I had been into Rocky Gulch with Ty and Genevieve a couple of times, but the city? Between the shooting schedule and my daily report for Bud and the perpetual ache in my joints and muscles, I hadn't had the time or mental capacity to even think about driving all the way to Fort Worth. That would have meant sacrificing an entire night's sleep.

Even I wasn't willing to pull an all-nighter just for some city time.

"We leave in ten," Ty said as he pushed back from the table.

I leaped to my feet. "I'll be ready."

Turning, I started to dash for the door, ready to race upstairs and change out of what had become my cowgirl uniform—worn in jeans, old cowboy boots, and a variety of tees and western shirts, all belonging to Genevieve. If I was going to the city, I was going in full-on Cassie gear. Black, black, and—oh yeah—black.

But I didn't get two strides from the table before my manners kicked me in the butt.

How could I leave a messy table? Especially when I knew it would only make cleaning up even harder later.

I turned back, stacked my silverware on my plate, and carried the pile over to the sink, next to Ty's. Then I returned to the table and grabbed the empty serving dishes while Ty gathered the glasses and mugs.

"Shoo," Genevieve said as I started rinsing the clean dishes. "You go get ready. I can handle this itty bitty mess."

Rather than leap at her release, I grabbed a dish rag and wiped off the kitchen table and the counters. Only when she started shooing me again did I finally relent.

By my calculations, I had about three minutes left. I was up the stairs in a matter of seconds, stripped down to my underthings in a minute later. When Ty called up that the bus was leaving, I only had my boots—normal, lace-up, city girl boots —left to pull on.

Rather than risk getting left, I grabbed them in one hand, my purse in the other, and raced back downstairs.

Ty laughed gently. "In a rush, city gal?"

I threw him a playful scowl.

"Put your boots on," he said. "I have to grab something from the office."

I was just tying the knot on my second boot when he returned to the front hall.

"Ready cowgirl?" he asked.

"As I'll ever be."

Genevieve emerged from the kitchen, apron-free and with a small purse slung over her shoulder.

"Y'all didn't think you would have all that city fun without me, did you?" she teased. A mischievous sparkle shone in her eyes.

"Not for a second," Ty said, holding the door open for us. He glanced at me. "I told you to hurry. We almost escaped."

I laughed.

Genevieve swatted him. "You can never escape me."

"A brother has to try." He winked at me as he turned and bounded down the porch steps. "I'm going to let Victor know to get the stall ready."

Eddie panned the camera to Ty as he jogged toward the bunkhouse.

Genevieve turned to me. "Don't you let us leave Fort Worth without taking you to Girabeaux's." Her face took on a dreamy expression. "Their molasses cheesecake is the best around."

I smiled and let her lead me to the truck. "Sounds heavenly."

Once again, I settled into the passenger seat, while Genevieve bounced into the back seat. Eddie climbed next to her as Ty returned. Even with his seatbelt on, Eddie managed to twist around and aim the camera at me and the cowboy as the truck backed away from the house.

I turned in my seat, to watch our progress, only to see the big curved face of a trailer filling the back window. How had I not even noticed that on the way out?

Oh right. I'd been too hyper-focused on the fact that we were actually going to the city.

Now that my initial excitement had—well, if not died down, then at least *calmed* down—I had to put my producer hat on. A four-hour drive through the nothingness of Texas did not make good television.

The truck hit a rut, jostling me up against the window.

"So...," I said, reaching for something that might make less-than-boring conversation, "was the decision to head into Ft. Worth a spur-of-the-moment one?"

Ty checked left before pulling out on the main road. "We get into the city at least a couple times a month. Usually when there's a livestock auction."

"Is that why we're going today?" I asked. "An auction?"

He nodded, but offered nothing further.

He had to give me more than a nod. "Is it a cattle auction?"

"No," he said, and I was afraid that was all he was going to say, until he added, "It's an equine auction."

"Equine," I replied, brilliantly. "So it's horses."

Again, a nod.

"Is that why we're bringing a trailer?"

"Yes."

The curt answers and the silence were killing me—and my chances of making decent entertainment. I thought about my conversation with Bud and about what I knew about making conversation look interesting. About what made the premise of this show appealing to potential viewers: contrast. People would turn in to *Try It On* to see the huge divide between my New York life and my attempt at a cowgirl one. To see the huge divide between me and Ty. And if Ty was going to give me strong and silent, I was going to have to give the camera a chatty, bubbly girl.

"I've been to auctions before," I said, beginning a ramble. "Art auctions, mostly. Sometimes antiques. My mother once bought an urn that she swore contained the ashes of Alexander the Great."

Eddie chuckled and it took all my restraint not to turn and glare at him—which would mean glaring at the camera.

Babbling was not in my normal repertoire, but if it got me closer to getting my career back on track, I'd make a fool of myself. Even more than I already had.

"My brother is being humble," Genevieve said from the back seat. "He goes to the auctions to save horses that others would just as soon slaughter."

A gasp burst out of me. "What?"

I looked from Genevieve to Ty and back again.

"It's a sad truth about the horse industry," Ty explained. "The old and unrideable ones are simply discarded."

"That's terrible." I shuddered. "What an awful thing."

"We have a pasture on the back forty," Genevieve added, "where the hay is plentiful and they can live out their days."

I hadn't known horses for long, but the few I'd met were

sweet, docile creatures. The idea that someone would kill one just because it had outlived its usefulness make my heart ache.

For several long minutes, I stared silently out the window and considered how I could work this into the show. Maybe use the show's high profile to raise awareness of this horrible practice. But no matter how I tried to play it, I came back to one thing: it wasn't entertaining. *Try It On* was entertainment, pure and simple. It wasn't a documentary or a public service announcement. It wasn't the venue for an exposé.

"Can we get some tunes going," Genevieve asked. "The sound of tires on pavement is going to get old real fast."

Ty turned on the radio and strains of country music filled the truck. Other than the sound of Genevieve humming along to the melody, we passed the rest of the drive in silence. If I couldn't work-in the dark side of the horse world, I could at least shine a light on Ty's efforts to make a difference.

I watched him from across the cab, his eyes trained on the road. Jaw set, like he was intent on taking on the world. Maybe he was. I was starting to believe that Ty Haywood was one of the best human beings I'd ever met. If only that didn't complicate my growing feelings for him even more.

FROM THE MOMENT I saw the first hint of the skyline, I was like a little girl on her way to the circus. All excitement and energy and bouncing around in my seat. It had been less than two weeks since Eddie and I drove through here on our way to the ranch, but it felt like a lifetime.

A lifetime without drive-thru coffee, morning traffic, and five-star dining.

"I need sushi," I blurted.

Ty laughed out loud. "You might need to look up the word *need* in a dictionary, city gal."

"No." I shook my head. "This is a legitimate need. If I don't get my regular fix of rice and seaweed I might literally go insane."

This time when Ty laughed, I laughed with him.

He had a way of smiling that broke open his whole face like a burst of sunshine. Even serious and scowling, he was a beautiful man. But smiling...? He was a whole other level of beautiful.

There I went with those complicated feelings again.

"What else are you looking forward to?" he asked. "What else is on your must do in the city list?"

"You joke," I replied, pulling out my phone and opening my notepad app, "but I really do have a list."

Ty nodded. "I expected nothing less."

"Look," I gasped. "Actual signal!"

My phone might actually work again.

Eddie snorted.

"First," I said, ignoring the back seat, "a drugstore."

"Something you couldn't get at the StarMart?"

My cheeks burned. "I need to restock my antacids and I need some...cream. I'm not used to sitting in a saddle."

Genevieve said the appropriate term was saddle sore. All I knew was that I ached in places that probably shouldn't exist.

I couldn't be certain, but I could have sworn Ty's cheeks darkened a little too.

He coughed awkwardly. "What else?"

"Socks," I said.

He lifted an eyebrow. "Socks?"

"For my boots." I lifted my knee to display my right boot. "I only packed one pair of tall socks. All the rest were footies."

"We have socks," Genevieve. "You're more than welcome to borrow a few pair."

I made a face which I was sure Eddie caught square in the center of the frame.

"I have a thing about socks," I explained. "I can share almost anything else, but I need my own socks."

She shrugged. "To each her own."

"That's it," I said, pocketing my phone. "Only three essentials."

Ty began, "Socks, sushi, and—"

"The drugstore," I answered quickly, not wanting to mention the cream for my saddle-sore cheeks again. "Yes. That's it."

It wasn't that having a sore backside was the most embarrassing thing on the planet, but it wasn't something I wanted to discuss in depth on camera. Or in person. Or ever. My mother would be mortified.

"What else is on our schedule?" I asked. "Besides the auction?"

"I need a new cowboy hat," Genevieve announced. "Since *someone* crushed mine under a horse hoof."

"You shouldn't have let it fly into the arena," Ty answered quickly. "Roughshod couldn't help it."

"I wasn't blaming the *horse*," Genevieve teased back.

She and I shared a look and I giggled when she winked at me. As an only child, I never experienced this kind of sibling banter. To be honest, I still didn't fully understand it. It was just something I had come to accept that I would never comprehend.

"Where do we get your hat?" I asked.

"We," Genevieve said, a huge smile in her voice, "are going to Buchanan's."

I lifted my brows. Was I supposed to know what Buchanan's was?

"It's the biggest western store in Fort Worth," Ty answered. "It has everything a cowboy—"

"Or cow*girl*," Genevieve interrupted.

"—could possibly need," Ty finished.

"Well, a *wannabe* cowgirl anyway," Genevieve amended. "It's also a bit of a tourist trap."

I smiled. "So no feed buckets or horse blankets?"

She shook her head.

"Hardly," Ty answered.

When I turned back to face the highway, I was stunned to see the city had crept up on us. A dozen skyscrapers loomed up into the blue. Not quite New York-worthy, but certainly enough to feed my city fix. As we exited the freeway and headed into the downtown, I rolled down my window and absorbed the sights and sounds of the city. Cars, buses, taxis, people, dogs.

It washed over me, recharging my depleted metro meter and making me feel like the time in the country was nothing but a bad dream.

Ty parked in a garage. We emerged on a wide plaza that was covered in fountains and people and cafe tables. It literally bustled with activity.

I could hardly contain a little leap of joy when I saw a coffee shop across the way.

Even Eddie seemed a bit lighter on his feet than usual.

"Why don't we hit Buchanan's together," Ty suggested,

"then we can split up for a while, I'll do my business at the auction, and then we meet back up for dinner."

"Dinner?" I asked breathlessly.

He jerked a hand over his shoulder. "There's a terrific Japanese place around the corner. They have mouthwatering Kobe beef."

I bit my lips, my eyes practically popping out of my sockets.

"And sushi," he said, with an exaggerated sigh.

I clapped and jumped up and down.

"Come on, city gal," Ty said, gesturing for us to follow. "Let's check out Buchanan's."

Genevieve linked her arm through mine. "You're going to love it," she said, sounding as excited about the western wear store as I had been about the prospect of sushi.

Eddie moved into position in front of us, turning around and walking backward so he could capture our conversation.

I would withhold my judgment about Buchanan's. But I couldn't imagine anything as wonderful as a well-made spider roll.

Two hours later, I was almost convinced. Buchanan's had been a wonderland of belts and blue jeans, buckles and chaps. Boots made from any and all leathers the animal world had to offer—and some I was pretty sure were completely made up. Cowboy hats in every color of the rainbow, including rainbow, glittered, and sequined.

Whether you were ready to ride out on the ranch or step out on the dance floor, Buchanan's had you covered.

I managed to find some boot socks that made my feet feel like they were cocooned in clouds and a wide leather belt with a star-covered buckle that wasn't truly necessary to keep

Genevieve's almost-too-tight jeans in place but that made me feel just a little bit more like a real cowgirl. My haul pretty minimal in comparison. Ty picked up few pairs of jeans, two pairs of work gloves, three shirts, and a weird wedge of wood that he called a boot jack.

Genevieve got two new hats—one, a soft dove gray that matched the blue and gray plaid shirt she'd lent me, and a straw one to replace the one Roughshod had crushed—a pair of concho earrings, and a long peasant skirt that flounced out in layers of ruffles.

Even Eddie got in on the shopping, picking up a pair of cufflinks for his boyfriend, a skinny necktie thing that the salesman called a bolo, and a wide leather cuff with a big turquoise oval in the center.

Genevieve was right. There was something for everyone at Buchanan's.

WHEN WE PARTED at the exit, Ty headed back for the truck to drop off the packages, Genevieve took Eddie to her favorite cupcake shop, and I looked up the nearest drugstore on my— yes, working!—phone.

The closest one was about six blocks away.

I figured I had better touch base with my city life while I had a signal, so as I started for the drugstore, I dialed Bethany's number. She and I had been friends since college and we always kept in touch. But since our stint on *One Straight Guy* we'd become closer than ever. She was the one person I knew would always be ready, willing, and able to listen and advise.

She answered on the second ring.

"Cassie, hi!" she exclaimed. "I've been trying to call you."

"Is something wrong?" I asked, concerned by her breathless tone.

"No, not at all," she cooed. "Chris and I are engaged!"

My face broke out in a grin. That certainly warranted some breathlessness. "Congratulations."

Despite the disaster that had been *One Straight Guy*, the show had actually had some wonderful results. Not the least of which was Bethany finding love with the show's supposedly-but-apparently-not-at-all gay chef, Chris. They'd moved in together a while back. It was only a matter of time before he put a ring on her finger.

Since I'd hooked her up with the job, I felt a sense of possibly-undeserved accomplishment for getting them together.

"I'm so happy for you," I said, meaning it.

"What about you?" she asked. "How is Texas?"

"Texas is…" I shrugged and looked helplessly around, as if I might find the words on the city streets. Instead, I found myself passing a gallery with some really interesting western-themed art on display. I paused to window-shop and answered, "It's different."

"I'll bet," she replied. "How's the show? It has to be going better than the last one."

True. But filming hadn't been the problem on *One Straight Guy*—too many straight guys had.

"You'll never guess what happened," I said, then finished before she could even try. "The idiotic princess didn't show."

"Oh no," she gasped. "Did you find a replacement?"

I groaned. "Yes."

"Who?"

"Guess."

She hesitated for only a second before figuring it out.

"*No.*" She choked on a laugh. "You? You're playing cowgirl?"

"None other."

She didn't even bother trying to hold back the next laugh. While she giggled uncontrollably in my ear, I studied a painting that depicts a landscape that looked like it could have been straight from the Black Willow. Only instead of the boring beige and blue that I saw on a daily basis, the artist represented the earth with rich, purple-hued grasses and the sky in burning shades of red and orange. It was an explosion of color. Did the rural landscape ever look that beautiful? All I had ever seen was dusty and boring.

"I'm sorry," Bethany said, finally getting herself back under control, "but that is just too funny. You, of all people."

I turned away from the window. "Don't I know it?"

"Huh," she said. "Now that I think about it, you might just be the perfect person for the show. I've never met anyone with less country in her soul."

"I take that as a compliment."

She laughed. "You would."

We chatted for a few more minutes, until I reached the drugstore and ducked inside to get my necessities. By the time I got to the restaurant, I was feeling seriously recharged. City time. Bethany time. And, I was a little ashamed to admit, quality smartphone time.

Maybe I needed to institute some unplugged time when I got back home. As much as I loved my technology, I didn't like feeling like I *had* to have access to it.

Everyone was waiting for me in the Japanese restaurant,

and Eddie had the camera all set up for the meal. *Samurai Sam's* wasn't anything like the elegant sushi place I visited at least once a week back home. It had a distinctly Texas twist, with walls covered in worn barn wood and a menu that included fajita rolls and jalapeño seaweed salad.

The only open seat was next to Ty—probably because it made filming easier for Eddie.

I dropped into the chair and reached for the menu.

"Think this place will satisfy your sushi fix, city gal?" Ty asked.

My mouth watered as I scanned the menu of familiar favorites and TexMex twists. "Oh, I think I'll find something to get me by until next time."

"Good evening, ma'am," our server said as he set down water and iced tea for my tablemates. "Can I get you something to drink?"

"Hot tea, please." I exchange a look with Ty. "Are we ready to order?"

He nodded and indicated that I should go first.

"I'll have a spider roll and a rainbow roll," I began. In addition to the traditional sushi, I wanted to try something unconventional. "And can you recommend one of the house specialty rolls?"

"The lady is from New York," Ty offered. "I believe she's looking for a taste of Texas."

The server beamed. "Then I suggest the Longhorn roll, ma'am. Seared Angus beef, fire roasted peppers, and avocado mousse."

"Sounds delicious." I closed my menu.

Genevieve ordered next, requested miso soup and a California roll. The sushi order of amateurs. But at least she was trying.

Eddie ordered the Longhorn roll and a Kobe filet with horseradish salsa.

Ty went last. "Can I get a spicy tuna nigiri, unagi maki, and the hamachi and Kobe platter?"

My jaw fell slack.

"Oh, and two orders of edamame for the table," Ty finished.

The server nodded enthusiastically. "Very good, sir."

While he had vacated to enter our order, I stared at Ty.

"What?" he asked, all innocence.

"Spicy tuna, unagi, and hamachi?" I asked, repeating back his order of raw tuna, freshwater eel, and yellowtail. "That's quite the sophisticated sushi order."

"For a cowboy?" He picked up his chopsticks and used them to gently lift a slice of pickled ginger from the dish at the center of our table.

It made me sound like a snob, but I said, "Well, yeah."

He just smiled. "This cowboy is full of surprises."

He certainly was. I smiled back as reached for my own slice of ginger.

NINE

WHEN I ROLLED out of bed Tuesday morning, my muscles didn't scream in aching agony. Either the day off over the weekend had given me a much-needed boost, or after more than two weeks on the ranch, they must have given up on my actually listening to them. I was betting on the latter. Could total system failure be far behind?

My brain, on the other hand, was singularly determined to stay asleep. Even after splashing cold water on my face several times giving my cheeks a good wake-up slapping, I could have fallen right back into bed and slept for another six hours. At least.

But the scream-barking coyote and my career had other plans.

So, instead of succumbing to the lure of my all-too-comfortable bed, I pulled on my work clothes and trudged down the stairs.

Genevieve was waiting for me at the bottom with a muffin and steaming cup of coffee.

"Ty's already at the pen," she said, shoving the breakfast offering at me. "He wants you to meet him there."

I grumbled something that might have been thank you and shuffled toward the back door. Eddie's heavy footsteps thudded after me.

The awareness of a camera documenting my every step made me stiffen my spine and lift my chin. If I was going to feel miserable, at least I could avoid *looking* miserable in front of thousands of future *Try It On* viewers. As I descended the porch steps, I straightened my spine and gave my head a good shake. Maybe I could shake the lazy away.

I followed the direction of Genevieve's vague gesture toward a small pen between the barn and the bunkhouse. The normally-empty pen currently contained several small calves.

My boots scuffed into the red dirt as I made my way along the worn path. Seriously, I was not built for hard labor. I was made for hiking city streets and climbing into taxis. My body was never going to forgive me for this punishing experience.

Eddie sped up a little so he could film me from a different angle.

And every last second was being caught on tape. Lucky me.

"Morning," I grumbled to Ty, leaning my arms—and my entire body weight—onto the fence.

"Can you bring me that blanket." He pointed at a thick red blanket sitting on the ground next to the gate. He didn't look up.

I grabbed the blanket and carried it inside to where Ty knelt next to a massive brown cow and smaller dark brown blob that looked like a jellyfish and a dog got into a fight. As I handed him the blanket, the jelly-dog moved, lifted its head and I could see that it was actually a baby calf. A brand new baby calf.

"Oh!" I slapped my hands over my mouth.

My mental fog evaporated in an instant.

The tiny little thing, covered in I-didn't-want-to-know-what-that-was goo, was about the most precious thing I had ever seen. A precious, soggy mess. Ty rubbed the blanket over its wet body. Its tiny head leaned into Ty's touch.

I wasn't what you would call maternal. Or girly. Or given to being emotional about anything that didn't involve physical pain. But as I looked at that brand new life, my eyes stung with threatening tears.

What I wouldn't have given to trade places with Eddie in that moment.

I hadn't actually been behind a viewfinder since film school. After the wrap of my thesis project—a disturbing documentary about the effects of wildfires on communities and the environment—I'd gotten an AP job with Go Gorman Studios and I'd been handling producer duties ever since. But my hands itched to adjust the aperture and shutter speed, to create that perfect formula of white balance and ISO that would capture the real-life experience as fully as possible for the viewer.

I looked over my shoulder to make sure Eddie was getting this all on film, then immediately checked myself for breaking the fourth wall. I had to behave like that camera wasn't there. One of the keys to reality television was making the audience believe they were watching real lives, unaffected by the presence of a sometimes-substantial camera crew in the room.

They could cut it out in editing, but every time I slipped into producer mode meant a stretch of unusable footage.

But in that moment, I didn't care about wasted tape or the fourth wall or staying in character. All I cared about was making sure the viewers got to see what I was seeing. A miracle.

I was transported back to film school, when my dream had been to make life-altering documentaries, emotional short films, and breathtaking indie movies. I'd never felt so far from that dream as I did in that moment. Producing reality television felt like a decade-long detour.

But that was a thought—and a personal debate—for another day. I had a job to do, and I was going to do it to the best of my ability.

"Are you, um…" I asked, trying to bring myself back into my role, "always present at a new birth?"

Ty shook his head. "Mostly the cattle can take care of it themselves." He pushed to his feet and wiped his hands on his jeans. "Clara here had a bit of trouble last time, so I've been keeping her up at the loafing shed as her time drew near."

The cow in question made a sad braying noise.

Ty patted her on the rump. "Didn't need me a bit, did you girl?"

Clara leaned down to inspect her newborn.

"How many has she had?" I asked, trying to remember that conversation made for good television.

"This one is her sixth."

"Six?" I nearly choked. "How many babies do cows usually have?"

Ty shrugged. "A dozen. Two, maybe, if they are healthy and well-maintained."

I shook my head in awe.

I sensed Genevieve walk up next to me.

"As an only child," I replied, "I find the idea of having that many siblings utterly terrifying."

Ty winked at me. "Even one can be a challenge."

"I heard that," Genevieve said as she leaned against the fence. "Clara came through okay?"

"Like a pro."

"It's amazing," I said, unable to take my eyes off the baby calf. "I've never seen a just-born anything."

The little calf made a tiny squeak and moved its legs closer to its body. The thing was only a few minutes old, but while we watched, it strained and struggled and finally pulled itself to its feet. It stood there, wobbly on tiny new legs, proud as a toddler taking its first steps.

Not that I knew anything more about toddlers than baby calves, but I could imagine.

"I just came out to remind you about dinner," Genevieve told Ty.

He winked at her. "I won't forget."

"See that you don't." She turned to me. "We're having our monthly all-hands dinner tonight. Don't let him stay out in the field until all hours."

"Yes ma'am."

As Genevieve turned to walk back to the house, Ty smiled. "Been here just over a week and already she's got you keeping tabs on me."

I laughed. "Hey, I know how to recognize a real boss when I see one."

He laughed out loud. "Fair point. Come on, city gal," he said as he climbed over the fence, "we have work to do."

But as Eddie and I followed him into the barn, I couldn't

help thinking about that baby calf. Or about my instinct to film those precious moments.

♥

EVERYTHING in the house was quiet, peaceful, as I sank into the bath. According to Ty, Genevieve's monthly all-hands dinner would be quite the affair. In addition to the Victor and Jesse, the men who work at the Black Willow, she also invited some friends from town and neighboring ranches.

Or, as he apparently liked to call it, "Everyone from here to kingdom come."

There was no way I could spend a night socializing still covered in the stench of horses and labor. I'd insisted on returning early enough to take a shower, but when I stepped into the bathroom the tub called to me.

Twenty minutes later, I was fairly certain the stink had soaked away. And my muscles were feeling better too.

"When I get back to civilization," I told myself, "I'm joining a gym. No more wobbly legs for this girl."

By the time I was dressed and towel-drying my hair in my bedroom, the silence from the floor below had gradually evolved into a dull roar of chatter and conversation. The sounds of several voices—none of which I could recognize through the muffling effects of the house—floated up the stairs.

Deciding to just let my curls fly free, I finger-combed my hair, popped in a pair of plain silver hoops, and stepped into my black studded flats. Bethany hadn't exactly agreed when I suggested the studs counted as an additional accessory, but she had approved the purchase.

Back in black jeans and a black V-neck tee, I felt more like myself than I had in days.

As I descended to the first floor, the voices got progressively louder. I rounded the corner into the kitchen and found an absolute melee of people.

There had to be at least dozen people crammed into the cozy space. More voices from the directions of the living and dining rooms told me there had to be close to twenty-five people in the house.

The Black Willow ranch big house felt more like a crowded subway car than a country oasis.

"Cassie," Genevieve shouted across the room. "Finally. I want you to meet Ashley and Emily."

She waved me over to her position by the stove. I had to wind my way through three different conversations—including one between the cute young ranch hand Jesse and a girl I recognized from the McLaren ranch, and another between three elderly ladies who were having an animated debate about the latest season of *Travel Wars*. Eddie was filming the debate.

I finally broke through the group, emerging into the kitchen like a marathoner crossing the finish line.

"Holy macaroni," I exclaimed as I caught my breath. "When you throw a party, you really throw a party."

Genevieve waved off my compliment. "Cassie, these are two of my best friends, Ashley and Emily Porter."

Babe sat at her feet, staring longingly at the huge bubbling pot on the stove.

I pushed my still-damp hair out of my face and blinked. The two girls in front of me were mirror images of each other

—long honey blond hair parted on opposite sides, matching double dimples, and heads tilted to opposite sides.

"I'm Emily," the one on with the left-side part said.

Right-side part smiled. "And I'm Ashley."

"Nice to meet you." I tucked a chunk of my hair behind one ear.

"We're twins," Emily said.

Ashley added, "Mirror twins."

"I'm the good one." Emily nodded at her sister. "She's the evil one."

"Don't believe a word," Genevieve intervened. "They're both evil."

"You can say that again," Ty boomed.

He walked up behind the twins and threw an arm around each girl's shoulders. They simultaneously leaned into his sides, looking up at him with honest-to-goodness stars in their eyes. I had a feeling there was some life-long crushing going on there.

He grinned innocently as they swooned against him.

I exchanged a look with Genevieve.

She bit back a smile and shrugged innocently. Ah, so clearly these were among the ladies she was trying to fix up with her brother.

From what I could tell, Ty was completely oblivious to the plan.

"How long until the soup is on?" he asked. He released the twins and turned to sniff the big pot that was the center of Babe's attention.

The big black beast sat up straighter as her owner lifted the lid. And then whimpered as the aroma of mouthwatering chili wafted out. He patted her absently on the head but made no move to give her even a taste.

"It's ready now," Genevieve answered. "If you would sound the gong, I'll start ladling."

"With pleasure." Ty lifted his hands to his mouth, magnifying his voice as he called out, "Supper time! Form an orderly line. You know we don't tolerate chaos here at the Black Willow."

"None at all?" I teased.

He winked at me. "Well, maybe just a little."

Some occupants of the kitchen laughed while others teased Ty about his definition of the word order. But this clearly wasn't their first dinner here at the ranch. Those already in the kitchen formed a line, streaming past a pile of bowls, grabbing one, and presenting it to Genevieve for a serving of her famous chili. The guests in the rest of the house filed in from other rooms, and soon the line was out the door.

"Here, you take this spot," a woman's voice said.

It was Sue-Anne, the owner of the Lone Star Bunkhouse—and one of the ladies who'd been having the *Travel Wars* debate in front of Eddie's camera. She motioned me to take the place in front of her in line.

"Oh no, I couldn't—"

"Nonsense," she said with a wave. "You're a guest."

I wanted to insist that we were all guests, but arguing didn't seem like the gracious thing to do. So I kept my mouth shut and accepted her offer.

"Thank you."

We shuffled forward, getting closer and closer to the stove.

I grabbed a bowl from the stack as I moved past. The body

in front of me, the young ranch hand Jesse, stepped up to Genevieve.

"Smells delicious as always," he said, ducking his head.

He moved on to join to girl from the McLaren ranch in the living room, and I held my bowl out for a serving. A little boy who couldn't have been more than five or six appeared out of nowhere in front of me.

"Can I have a bowl, Miss Genevieve?"

"You need to wait your turn, Austin," she told him with a patient smile. "It's not polite to cut in line."

His little face fell.

"You know what?" I said, handing him my bowl. "Sue-Anne was nice enough to give me her spot. It's only right that I pay it forward."

Both Austin and Genevieve beamed at me, and I couldn't tell which smile was brighter. While she scooped a big ladle of chili into his bowl, I moved back to the end of the line and grabbed a new one. By the time I made it back to the stove and got my serving, it seemed like every possible seat in the house was taken.

Genevieve grabbed her bowl and ended up sitting on the arm of the couch in the living room. Eddie stood in the corner by the fireplace, his camera resting on the mantle while he downed spoonfuls of chili. Babe sat at his feet—or maybe even on his feet—waiting for even a morsel to drop.

The roar of the conversation was practically deafening and it seemed like everyone with engaged in some kind of loud, enthusiastic debate with everyone else.

I'd never been claustrophobic a day in my life, but between the density of voices and bodies, I suddenly had to get out of there. I slipped back into the kitchen and out onto the back porch.

Once outside, I drew in a deep breath of fresh.

"You escaped," Ty's voice said from the shadows off to my right.

I whirled around and squinted into the darkness. "So did you."

He stepped forward until I could make out his silhouette against the light streaming through the back door. "I can only tolerate mass gatherings for so long."

"Yeah," I said, turning as he joined me at the railing, "it's a lot to take."

"I thought you city gals loved a good crowd?"

I scooped a spoonful of chili toward my mouth. "There are crowds, and then there are *crowds*. I don't go to Times Square at New Year's either."

My lips closed around the spoon and the delicious flavor of Genevieve's chili hit my tongue. If someone had bottled the flavor of what Texas felt like, of what working on the Black Willow felt like, this chili was it.

"Oh my God," I said around another mouthful. "This is amazing."

"Don't go telling the cook," Ty said. "She'll get a big head."

"Our little secret."

As we stood there, looking out over the Black Willow, with a star-filled sky twinkling above, I was hard-pressed to remember a more perfect moment. Maybe there was something to the country life after all.

TEN

WHEN THE HOUSE phone rang the next morning, I knew instinctively it was Bud, even before Genevieve called out, "Cassie, it's for you."

My heart thudded in my chest. I'd been giving it my all for the last week and a half, literally putting everything on the line in the name of becoming a true cowgirl. I hadn't always succeeded, but trying had to count for something.

I didn't hear back from New York on any of the dailies, so I had assumed that no news meant good news. Now, as my blood pressure soared, I wondered if that was self-delusion.

As much as I didn't really care about whether or not I pulled off the cowgirl act, I *did* really care whether the show got the green light. And to do that, I had to pull off the cowgirl act. Which meant I had to act like I cared whether or not I pulled off the cowgirl act. It was a vicious circle.

So, with every fear and feeling of desperation I had beating out a rhythm in my throat, I picked up the receiver.

I glanced across the kitchen, where Ty stood at the sink, his back to me, washing a stack of dishes from last night's epic dinner.

"This Cassie."

"Please hold for Mr. Gorman," Bud's assistant said.

My fingers drummed an unsteady beat on the kitchen table.

Waiting did nothing to calm my nerves. In fact, they only escalated as I waited. Waited. Waited.

Eddie reached across the table with the hand that wasn't holding the camera to his shoulder and stilled my fidgeting.

Finally, Bud came on the line.

"We just got done previewing the new tape," he said without preamble.

"Yes, s—Mr. Gorman," I breathed.

I knew that *we* meant the executive board at the production company and whatever focus groups they had polled. Bud was at the top, but there were several vice presidents and heads of development that would need to weigh in on the show in order to move things forward. As president, Bud could strong-arm a project into production. The risk was high, though. If he was wrong, if he supported one too many failures, he would be in my exiled shoes in no time.

Bud cleared his throat.

I held my breath.

"Better," he said gruffly, as if the praise literally hurt him. "Much better."

I sighed out with all of my being. "Thank you, sir."

Eddie gave me a questioning thumbs up. I returned the gesture.

"But," he said, bursting my bubble of relief immediately, "it's still missing something."

I cast my gaze to the ceiling. What more could I do? I'd tried anything and everything, I'd humiliated myself in every way. What else was there?

"Do you remember the number one rule of marketing?" he asked.

I wracked my brain for what the rule might be. For the life of me—for the life of my career—I couldn't remember.

When I didn't answer, he did. "Sex sells, Bishop."

"Sex, sir?" I couldn't help the slip back to calling him sir any more than I could help the blush that burned up my cheeks.

Eddie darted a glance around the camera, eyes wide.

I flicked a glance at the sink.

Maybe I was imagining things, but I swore Ty's shoulders straightened a little. Well, at least he couldn't have heard Bud's statement.

I kept my voice low as I asked, "What do you mean?"

"I mean, you and the cowboy," he explained. Thank goodness Ty's back was to me or I would have burst straight into flames. "The ladies in the focus group thought he was..." Bud cleared his throat again, this time uncomfortably. "Delicious. Play that up."

Ty couldn't know what I was talking about, but I still felt the need to keep quiet.

"Play it up?" I echoed in a barely audible whisper.

"You know what I mean. Flirt more. Make eyes at the man." Bud paused and I could hear him shifting in his big executive chair. "The sparks are there every time you look at him. Turn them into fireworks for the camera."

I looked at Ty, who had shed his work shirt for the T-shirt underneath. His muscles bunched and rippled as he scrubbed the stack of plates and glasses. Who knew that a man washing dishes was one of my personal fantasies?

My gaze scanned lower, over his perfectly-worn jeans to the scuffed boots at his feet.

I fanned myself.

Gorman was right about one thing, there was definitely a spark of something within me when I looked at Ty. And if exploiting that spark was what it took to get this pilot made to Gorman's satisfaction, could I do it?

Even if I could… should I?

My brain tuned out the rest of Bud's conversation, instead buzzing with this new directive. *Fireworks for the camera.* Fireworks. With Ty.

Fireworks with Ty didn't seem like such a bad idea, but the thought of forcing them—or using them—for the show felt a little ethically squidgy.

He chose that moment to turn around. Grabbing a towel and a stack of wet bowls, he started carefully drying each one.

I closed my eyes and took a deep breath. Yes, I knew the sparks were there. On my side, anyway. In the way my heart raced a little faster and my skin heated a little more every time he stepped into the room.

But that was as far as I had let my attraction go. Ty was a die-hard Texan, a cowboy to the core, despite his stint in the city all those years ago. I was as city girl as they came. Anything between us couldn't have been anything more than a fling, a brief flash that would be over as soon as the shooting wrapped and I went back to the city.

It couldn't be more than that.

It couldn't be fireworks. Not really. Not for the long haul

But could I exploit them for the sake of the show? For the sake of my career?

"Do you understand me, Bishop?" Bud barked, and I knew he must have had to repeat his question.

"Sorry sir," I said, forcing my brain back into focus. "You cut out there for a second. What did you say?"

"I said," he grumbled, "either the next set of videos shows some sizzle between you and the cowboy, or the board is shutting down the production. Do you understand?"

An ultimatum. Either I get those fireworks on camera, or I pack up my bags—and my career.

"Yes sir," I said as a deep cloud of foreboding settled in over me. "I understand."

Then the line went dead. Bud was gone and I had my orders.

I walked back over to the base and hung up the phone.

"Everything okay?" Ty asked.

"What did they think of the latest tape?" Eddie asked. "Better?"

"Oh yes," I said, taking a moment too long to gather myself before turning back to face the guys. "Much better."

Eddie's camera was trained on me, and I pasted a big smile on my face that I hoped didn't look like some kind of serial killing cheerleader.

Ty didn't seem to notice anything off as he set the stack of dry bowls into a cabinet and then hung up his towel. I leaned back against the counter.

Eddie, however, wasn't fooled. He scowled and quirked his head in a questioning gesture. I frowned back and shook my head. It was bad enough to listen to Bud telling me to heat things up with Ty while the cowboy himself was standing in the room. At least he hadn't been able to hear Bud's side of the conversation.

I wasn't about to spell it out in neon red letters while he was in earshot.

"I need to call in an order at the feed store," Ty said, moving across the room. "Then we'll make a run into Rocky Gulch to pick up supplies."

I nodded awkwardly. Eddie gave him a thumbs up.

The moment Ty was out of the room, Eddie asked, "What?"

I forced myself to remain standing when all I wanted to do was sink dramatically back into the chair opposite Eddie and bang my head against the table's worn surface nine or ten times.

"The board thinks the action looks a lot better," I said.

Eddie nodded. "But…?"

"But," I conceded, "they think we need more sex appeal."

"More sex appeal?" Eddie asked, skeptical. "How on earth are you supposed to make ranch work—oh."

His gaze darted to the door Ty had just walked through. When he looked back at me, his eyes were wide… with excitement.

"Oh," he repeated, with an exaggerated facial expression. *"The cowboy."*

I nodded.

"You," he said, "and the cowboy."

I held my hands over my face and nodded again.

Eddie let out a low whistle.

This was one of those moments that film school professors often harped on and film students rarely thought worthy of their study. The ethics of going against your own instincts, interests, and maybe even beliefs, in order to get the shot.

Sure, I felt the pull of attraction between myself and Ty. But in any other situation, under any other circumstances, I would never, ever think to act on that. I would remind myself that nothing longer than the duration of filming was possible and it would be too messy to get involved with a cast member.

Of course, that was before my career depended on making this pilot work and before I became a cast member myself. All those ethical lines got blurry the moment I stepped in front of the camera and became part of the story.

I was literally between a rock and a hard place. Okay, not literally, but it was a rough spot. Either I swallowed my principles and capitalized on the attraction between me and Ty for the purposes of entertainment and profit, or I kissed my career in television goodbye without so much as a see you later.

I'd spent too many years on this path to let it vanish in a poof of conscience.

I shook my head. "How am I supposed to carry this off?"

"Haven't you ever flirted with a guy before?"

I threw him an irritated look. "Not on camera. Not when I wouldn't otherwise waste the time."

"Waste the time?" Eddie gave me a *tsk*ing worthy of my mother. "Don't you find the cowboy hot?"

"I'm not blind." I crossed my arms over my chest. "I just mean that in less than two weeks I'll be back in New York, and he'll still be here."

Eddie approached, the camera still perched on his shoulder and the red light blazing. "You don't have to propose marriage," he advised. "There's nothing wrong with a little harmless flirting."

Harmless being the keyword. Maybe that was my concern, that the flirting wouldn't be nearly as harmless as I wanted it to be. Maybe I would wind up feeling more for Ty than I wanted to feel. More than I could afford to feel.

"And," Eddie continued, "there's nothing wrong with a little wild west booty call."

I choked on my own tongue.

"It's the twenty-first century, Cassie-bear," he teased. "You're allowed to have a little fun."

Only the still-rolling camera kept me from blurting out the words racing through my mind. It didn't stop me from flipping him off.

Eddie knew how much was riding on this show. Fun wasn't even in the same time zone.

THE MOMENT I climbed into Ty's pick-up for the drive into Rocky Gulch I knew it was going to be the most awkward ride ever.

I plopped onto the passenger seat like usual. Then realized that there was at least four feet of space between us and there was nothing sexy about empty space. But how could I inch myself closer without seeming obvious about inching closer and without climbing onto the center console?

Every time the truck hit a bump in the road, I exaggerated the effect and bounced myself a little closer to Ty. One mile down the road and I couldn't see that I'd made any progress.

When I heard Eddie snort, I knew I must have looked like an idiot, too.

Time for another tactic.

Come on, Cassie, I told myself in a mental pep talk. *You know how to talk to guys. Just… be natural.*

"So, Ty," I asked, twisting to face him as much as the seatbelt would allow, "what are we getting at the feed store?"

His mouth quirked up to one side. "A few sacks of grain, menthol ointment, and dewormer."

"Ohhh," I said, trying to sound impressed.

But seriously, was there anything sexy about grain and ointment? There were probably few things *less* sexy than dewormer.

"What is the ointment for?" I asked, hoping for something I could use.

"We rub it on sore muscles," he said, "and on our stallion's nose so he can't smell the mares in heat."

Another snort from Eddie. For a cameraman who was supposed to remain all-but-invisible in the process, he sure did make his presence known often enough. I kept myself from throwing him a sharp glare—not for the intrusion, but for the judgment.

Up the sizzle attempt number one? Failure.

Clearly conversation was not my best tactic. I bit my lip and kept silent for the rest of the drive.

BY THE TIME we got to town, I was convinced that I really didn't know how to talk to guys. I'd never considered myself terribly awkward around people. But after twenty minutes of tension-filled near-silence, I had to reconsider the belief that I was a socially-functioning adult.

Ty pulled the truck into a gravel parking lot next to a big

metal building. A raised concrete platform, about three feet off the ground that looked kind of like a loading dock, ran along the entire front side. He backed up so that the truck's bumper was just a few feet from the edge.

"How often do you come into town?" I asked, following Ty up the steps to the main entrance of the feed store.

He pulled open the door and stepped back, gesturing me inside.

"A couple times a week," he replied. "Genevieve likes to hit up the farmer's market on Saturday's and we always end up needing something from either here or the hardware store."

See, I *could* manage conversation.

"So you're not completely devoid of social interaction." I flashed him a grin as I walked past him.

"Morning, Ty," a slightly pump blond woman called out from behind the counter.

She must have been pushing sixty and wore a hot pink tee that proclaimed *I'm not a cougar, I'm a panther*.

He pocketed his Yankee's cap. "Morning, Philly."

"You on the news or something?" she asked, nodding toward Eddie who was following us inside with the camera perched on his shoulder.

"No ma'am," he replied. "You remember Gen signed me up for that reality show. This here is Cassie, the producer, and her cameraman Eddie."

"Nice to meet you, Ms. Philly." I walked up to the counter and extended a hand.

"Just Philly," she said, eschewing my hand to pinch my left cheek. "Are you from Hollywood?"

"New York," I answered.

"You'd best watch out," she said with a wink, "or Ty here will sweet talk you into giving up your city life."

I laughed a little too loud before I remembered that I was supposed to be acting like that was exactly what was happening. I smiled at her, knowing that Eddie was right over my shoulder, catching it all on film. "Has he done that before?"

Philly flicked her gaze at Ty, who was studying a display of big white spray bottles under a sign that proclaimed an all-natural fly repellent.

"Doesn't even have to try." Philly's eyes went all dreamy, despite the ring on her left hand and the three decades—at least—that separated her from Ty. "The girls all fall in line behind him anyway." She stood up straighter. "Don't they Tyson James?"

He looked up, equal parts confused and concerned. "Don't they what, ma'am?"

"Exactly," she said dismissing him. "His sister and I have been trying to get him hitched ever since he got back to town. None of them took. But we keep trying."

I didn't know how to respond to that, so I just nodded. Did I have a sign on my forehead that said, *Please tell me more than you should probably tell a complete stranger?*

"I'll bet Genevieve's got her eyes set on you, now," Philly said, pushing away from the counter as if that was the end of the conversation.

I joined Ty at the back of the store, where he was reading the contents of a big tub. I picked up another one and read along.

"*Joint Health Helper*," I read out loud. "Is that like glucosamine for horses?"

Ty gave me a wry sideways glance. "Something like that."

He set the tub back on the shelf and moved on.

Great. My tactics were so not working.

I had to do something to get his attention. Something that Eddie could catch on camera that would make Bud, the executive board, and the focus groups happy.

But how did I get Ty to look at me as something other than this crazy city slicker who was making a fool of herself by trying to play cowgirl? I hadn't done much flirting in the last decade or so. By the time I got to film school, my social life had become more of a blurred spillover from my work life. The few dates and relationships I'd had grew out of projects and productions. More of the hey-want-to-get-drinks-after-work kind of situation.

I hadn't flirted to get a guy's attention since college.

I thought back to what flirting had been like back then. Often it took place at a frat party or in a bar where they hadn't looked too closely at my fake ID. Bethany and I spent most of those nights watching other girls make fools of themselves to get guys to look at them.

One of my suite-mates, Isobel Kendrick, an art history major with dual US and British citizenship, had been the master. She probably didn't need to try as hard as she did. Between her dark red curls, hypnotic eyes, and soft accent, guys tripped over each other to meet her. Still, she had an entire arsenal of flirting tactics. Her favorite had been the stumble-catch. It sounded like something out of a Hollywood RomCom, but it worked every time.

Guys like to play the hero, she'd said.

Oh God, I couldn't do that. I couldn't humiliate myself—more than I already had, anyway—just to get the fireworks on camera. Could I?

I glanced at Eddie, who leaned out from behind the camera just long enough to give me an imploring look. He wasn't begging for himself—his career wasn't on the line if this show totally tanked, but mine was.

For the sake of my career, I would shove the niggle of guilt to the back of my brain and give the stumble-catch a try.

As innocently as possible, I walked toward Ty's location, casually feigning interested in a five-foot-high pyramid of stacked orange canisters that proclaimed the contents to be a tasty, long-lasting horse treat. I glanced over my shoulder. Ty was reaching for a big green can of menthol ointment. In an instant, his hands would be full and the stumble-catch wouldn't work. I had to act fast.

I gritted my teeth, closed my eyes, and took half a step in his direction. As I moved, I let my right foot catch behind my left.

It almost worked.

I stumbled as planned. My arms flailed. Ty dropped the ointment and tried to catch me.

He missed.

I was too far away—geometry had never been my best subject—and instead of falling into his embrace, I went sailing into the shelf of ointment.

My combined weight and momentum were too much for the shelves, and they buckled, sending tins of ointment, bottles of oil, and jars of salve crashing to the floor. In a desperate attempt to catch myself, I kicked out—forgetting that I had one foot stuck behind the other.

Like a total freak, my tangled feet connected with the pyramid of canisters, sending the horse treats flying and rolling across the floor.

Up the sizzle attempt number two? *Epic* failure.

By the time we got back to the ranch, my wrist was in a bandage, my pride was unsalvageable, and I had given up completely on Bud's request to up the sizzle on the show. Clearly I was incapable of flirting without making myself look like a horse's rear. Flirting was not what I'd signed up for.

Then again, I hadn't signed up for being on the show at all, but that was beside the point now.

Besides, the idea of exploiting my attraction to Ty, of maybe using any reciprocal feeling him might have felt for me, left me with a heavy pit in my stomach that no amount of antacids could erase. It was manipulative and I hated manipulative people. I didn't want to hate myself.

The moment Ty put the truck in park, I flew out the door and around to the back.

"What first?" I asked Ty.

He looked at me, a little startled. Okay, so maybe I was being a bit over-the-top-excited, but I needed to recover some of my dignity after the feed store disaster that should thereafter be called the GCPDRG—the Great Can Pyramid Debacle of Rocky Gulch. And the best way to do that was to dive head-first back into the work.

He shook his head and said, "We need to move the grain into the barn. I'll call up Victor and Jesse—"

Before he could finish, I had the tailgate down and was dragging a giant sack of grain toward me. The truck bed was smooth enough that I had little trouble getting the sack to the edge, with half of it hanging off the end.

Eddie moved into position to get the best angle. He probably expected me to embarrass myself again. I resisted the urge to flip off the camera again. I was furious at myself for the flirting disaster, and an angry star always made for good television. For a viewer who wasn't me, anyway.

"Careful," Ty warned, "those things weigh fifty pounds."

"I got this," I insisted. "I used to carry sandbags in film school. I have a method."

I squatted down so that my shoulder was level with the tailgate, leaned forward and positioned myself under the bag, and then stood back up, lifting the bag as I rose. It only took me a moment to get my footing. Back in film school, I would carry two bags on each shoulder to balance my load.

To the naked eye I might have looked a bit scrawny, but I had muscle on my bones. And I wasn't afraid to use it.

Ty moved next to me and I tensed, expecting him to try to take my load from me.

Instead, he just reached in and grabbed another bag, hefted it onto his own shoulder—without having to do my little scoot-underneath move—and then started for the barn. I bit back a smile as I followed him.

In no time, we had all the grain in the feed room, the ointment in the wash bay, and the dewormer in the fridge in the break room.

"Nice work, city gal," Ty said with a wink. "We might just make a cowgirl out of you yet."

I beamed. "What next?"

"There is a children's horse show at the Four Seasons Fair tomorrow." Ty started for the aisle. "We need to get the girls ready."

"The girls?" I asked, falling in step beside him.

"The mares," he explained. "I always take them to the fairs so the littlest ones have something to ride."

The two stalls at the end of the barn housed DaisyDay and

LucyLoo, a pair of older horses that Ty claimed were the two gentlest creatures ever put on this earth. I grabbed the vertical bars of DaisyDay's stall.

"What kind are they?" I asked.

DaisyDay was white with black spots, a bushy mane, and soft brown eyes that practically begged for a carrot or a sugar cube. LucyLoo was shorter, a mottled mix of nearly white and golden beige, and she was as furry as a teddy bear.

"Lucy is an old Shetland pony and Daisy here's an Appaloosa." Ty grabbed the red halter from the hook outside Daisy's stall and drew the door open. "Come on. You can practice haltering."

My smile faltered. Sure, I had been riding Roughshod off and on for almost two weeks—as much off as I could convince Ty to let me have—but he had always done the haltering and saddling and pretty much everything else. He had instructed me and even walked me through a step or two, but in the end, all I'd really had to do was get over my fear and climb up on the horse.

Actually putting a halter on all by myself was something my courage wasn't quite prepared to face.

But just then DaisyDay swung her big head my way and stared at me. Not in a confrontational, don't-even-think-about-it way, but like are-you-going-to-save-me-from-this-horrible-stall-prison-or-not.

Pulling my teeth between my lips, I stepped into the stall.

Ty handed me the halter. "You remember what I showed you?"

I nodded. First, I unbuckled the strap on the side of the halter. Then I slipped my hand throughout the circular part in the front.

"It's okay," I whispered to DaisyDay as I approached. "I'm just going to slip this thing over your face. Nice and easy. You've done this a million times before."

I didn't tell her that I never had.

DaisyDay blinked at me. She didn't move a muscle as I placed the circular part over her nose and mouth.

"Good," Ty encouraged. "You're doing great."

I pushed up on my toes and tried to slip the other strap behind her ears. But I wasn't tall enough. I could only get it to just above her eyes.

"Here." Ty stepped up behind, and I felt the heat of his body along the length of mine.

My thoughts immediately turned to snow.

"Tickle her chin just here." He reached around my left side and scratched DaisyDay under her lip. She immediately dipped her head. At the same time, he used his right hand to guide mine, the one that held the halter, up and over her ears.

I should have been worried about the twelve-hundred-pound animal in front of me or the cameraman filming every terrifying moment through the bars in the stall wall or my career or the show. But all I could think about was how Ty had basically wrapped himself around me, pinning me between DaisyDay and his body.

His scent—a mix of man and hay and a hint of cologne or aftershave—stood out above the less pleasant smells in the barn around me.

With his hand still over mine, he guided me down to the buckle that hung loose below DaisyDay's ear. "One last step."

My body went into some kind of autopilot. I reached up with my other hand to grab the dangling strap, slid it up through the buckle, and secured the halter in place.

Ty dropped his hand and stepped back. "A perfect ten."

I blinked for a moment, trying to figure out what he meant. Then it hit me. I had haltered a horse. *I* had haltered a *horse*!

Pride washed over me. I spun around, a huge grin spread across my face. "I did it!"

Ty's pride showed in his matching grin. Before I knew what I was doing, I had swung my arms around his neck and was hugging him tight.

"I did it," I repeated. "I really did it!"

The moment Ty's hands slid to my waist, the reality of the situation hit me. I was full on hugging cowboy Ty, while Eddie's camera rolled, catching every moment for posterity—and future broadcast. And Ty was hugging me back.

Without even trying, without any flirting or machinations or desperately-disastrous tactics, I had somehow managed to make a step in the direction of Bud's directive.

Still, it felt weird to have this special, joyous moment captured on film. Like it was too personal to share. I gave Ty one last squeeze and then stepped out of his embrace.

"You haltered her like a pro," he said as he shoved his hands into his back pockets.

I smiled. "Lucky for me," I said, "I have a great teacher. What's next?"

"Ready to try Lucy?"

"You know it."

Because she was so much shorter, I managed to get Lucy into her green halter without needing Ty's help. But something in me still wished he had stepped in to show me how in the same way. I couldn't get the sensation of his body wrapped around me out of my mind. I couldn't stop fantasizing about ways to get him to do it again.

Then again, if I couldn't even pull off the stumble-catch without injuring myself and destroying half a feed store, it was highly unlikely that I would be able to finagle a situation in that would require close body contact with Ty.

But that didn't stop my imagining.

ELEVEN

"YOU CAN'T WEAR jeans to the Four Seasons Dance," Genevieve insisted as she dragged me into her room Friday afternoon.

"Why not?"

She didn't bother to respond.

"Not even light blue ones?"

"Not even light blue ones."

When she had knocked on my door thirty seconds ago and seen me sporting clean versions of what had become my daily uniform, she shook her head and grabbed my hand. I had a feeling things were only going to go downhill from there.

"Are you *sure* going to a dance is part of cowgirl life?" I asked skeptically.

"It is in Rocky Gulch." She walked over to her closet and pulled open the door. "I'm thinking something floral in with a lot of green."

Color *and* flowers? I suppressed a shudder.

As she slid clothes to the side, I glanced over my shoulder

at Eddie. From the big grin on his scruffy face, half-obscured by the camera, I could only guess he was enjoying my torture.

I didn't wear dresses. Slacks, pants, khakis, jeans. On the very rare occasion a knee-length skirt with a pair of thick tights and, that one time in high school, a pair of spandex leggings. All in black. But dresses were not in my wardrobe.

Introducing blue and gray had only been a recent, since-I-arrived-at-the-ranch development. I wasn't ready for colorful floral dresses.

"Ah, yes"—Genevieve pulled out an admittedly pretty sundress—"this is perfect."

Pretty for someone who wasn't me.

"It has ruffles," I observed.

Her smile was positively wicked. "It does."

I tried to back away, but she was too fast. Her hand clamped around my wrist and I was caught.

An hour later, Eddie had long since been shooed away—me in my underthings was *not* going on camera—and had left in search of something to eat. I was completely made over, my hair hung in loose finger-combed curls, and despite an endless string of protestations I was wearing the frilly floral dress.

I had to admit, the soft cotton felt nice breezing over my skin. But there was just way too much skin showing for my taste. Genevieve insisted, though. Not only would I fit in better —*everyone* would be in dresses, she'd said—but it was more fun to dance in a dress. That remained to be seen.

Then again, it also remained to be seen if I was actually going to dance at this dance. My vote was leaning toward no.

Then Genevieve confused me by pulling a pair of cowboy boots out of her closet.

Unlike the rough, sand-colored ones I'd been wearing,

these were shiny walnut brown. They were the last thing I would think to pair with the girly garment.

"Really?" I asked. "With a sundress?"

She beamed. "Trust me."

I should have been frightened of the glint in her dark blue eyes, but for some reason I did trust her.

When we walked downstairs, arm in arm, Ty, Eddie, and Babe stood at the bottom watching. Well, Babe sat, but she was staring up at me like had bacon in my boots.

I knew Eddie's camera was on me, but I could *feel* Ty's gaze. He skimmed it over the tiny straps at my shoulders, the ruffles and buttons on the bodice, the full skirt and the frilly hem. When he reached my feet, his dimples broke out.

And the Oscar goes to Genevieve. She had been right about the boots.

Next to me, she wore an almost matching outfit, with a different floral sundress and a pair bright red boots. I was dark where she was blond, pale where she was tan, but we looked like we belonged together.

I looked like I belonged in this country world.

"Don't you ladies clean up well?" Ty teased as we reached the ground floor.

His sister swatted him on the arm.

"Are we ready to go?" he asked.

"Absolutely," Genevieve said. She lifted her brows. "Eddie was thinking we should go in two cars."

"Why?" Ty asked, turning to look at him.

Eddie winced and I thought I saw Genevieve's boot heel leaving his sneaker.

"Um, yeah," Eddie said, shaking out his foot. "I thought it would be good to film the truck on the drive into town."

What was wrong with him? It was at least twenty minutes to Rocky Gulch. Twenty minutes of dust flying up from the truck's tires? Now that was thrilling television.

"That makes no sense," I replied. "We'll all ride together."

There, that settled it.

Fifteen minutes later, sitting in the truck next to Ty with Eddie and Genevieve following in her car, I had no idea how my directorial instruction had been so wholeheartedly ignored.

"Your sister is a piece of work," I said as we turn onto the main road into town.

"That she is," Ty agreed. "It's best not to fight her. She always gets her way."

I smiled and rode along in a peaceful silence for a few minutes.

I tugged at the hem of my dress—partly out of awkward nerves, but partly out of the fact that *I was wearing a dress*! For some inexplicable reason, I had actually gotten used to being on camera. Having Eddie film every last embarrassing and humiliating moment of my time as a cowgirl didn't bother me at all.

But put me in a dress, alone in a truck with a hot cowboy and I felt more like a high schooler with a crush than a grown woman with a soon-to-be-successful-again career.

Suddenly the silence got too awkward to bear. "Tell me about the Four Seasons Dance."

"We have one every season," Ty explained. "It's mostly an excuse for the citizens of Rocky Gulch to get together to socialize and gossip."

"Do they really need an excuse?"

Ty laughed and a warm feeling settled into my chest.

In the distance, the red glow of the setting sun outlined the buildings of Rocky Gulch.

"It kicks off a weekend festival," he continued. "Tomorrow there's the fair and a crafts market to raise money for the Rocky Gulch Scholarship Fund."

"Scholarship fund?" I echoed.

He nodded. "That's how I wound up at City College. The town paid part of my tuition."

"Wow, that's amazing," I said, half wishing Eddie was here to get that on film.

"Well, that," he said, "and I'd been hell-bent on getting out of this dusty town, out of this dusty state, my entire life. I jumped at the chance."

His voice trailed off a little at the end, like it was weighed down by sadness.

I knew from the article in the dossier and from what Genevieve said that their parents had died on their way back from taking Ty to the airport. And that then he had come home to help run the ranch after that. Genevieve felt guilty for him coming home. I wondered if he felt guilty for leaving in the first place.

I didn't ask any follow-up questions. Prying more into the personal affairs of the Haywood family was not on my agenda.

Luckily I was saved from further conversation as the truck rolled into town. Strings of red, white, and blue pennant banners hung across the streets. There were dozens of people walking along the sidewalks, chatting and laughing and enjoying the early evening.

It was exactly the picture-perfect vision of small town life.

Ty pulled the truck into a parking spot on a side street. Genevieve's parked right behind us.

"Are you ready for a real country dance?" Ty asked as he opened his door.

With that smile and those dimples, how could I say no?

THE FOUR SEASONS Dance was held in something called an ice house—which, from what I could tell, was basically Texas speak for a bar. Inside the metal building, strings of lights hung across the ceiling, Lone Star flags lined the walls, and country music poured from speakers scattered around the space.

Eddie headed into the crowd, either to shoot footage of the party scene or snag some treats from the bake sale table in the back corner whose sign proclaimed *Homemade Pralines and Pecan Pie*. Probably both.

Genevieve led us to a table near the front door, where a pair of older ladies manned a sign-in sheet and a box of pin-on stars.

"Good evening, Miss Emmeline," she said to the women, "Miss Janine."

"Genevieve Haywood," the woman on the left said. "How y'all doing?"

"Just fine," she replied. "This is Cassie Bishop." She reached back and tugged me toward the table. "She's here filming that TV show I was telling y'all about."

"Oh yes," the one on the right cooed. "Bringing so much excitement to our small town here."

"She's definitely shaken up things out at the Black Willow," Ty said from behind us.

He was close enough that I felt his breath on my bare

shoulder. A shiver raced down my spine. I smiled, a little embarrassed by the compliment—at least, I thought it was a compliment.

"Y'all better hurry," the woman on the left warned, "they're about to start the dance-off."

"D-dance-off?" I croaked.

Genevieve turned on me, a royal blue star in her hand and a mischievous smile on her face. "It's a Rocky Gulch tradition."

As she reached for my shoulder, intent on pinning the star to my borrowed dress, I had a bad feeling about what she was going to say.

"I don't dance," I blurted.

"That's just fine," Genevieve said, smoothing the star into place, "because my brother is a brilliant dancer."

With that, she grabbed me by both shoulders, spun me around, and gave me a little push toward Ty. His dimples were showing, but I could see the hesitation in his eyes.

"You don't have to," I whispered.

His smile softened.

"Neither do you," he whispered back.

I could have walked away. Maybe should have. Eddie wasn't filming this, it wasn't about making good television. It was about whatever connection was sparking between us. Which was exactly why I should have thanked him for letting me off the hook and headed off to the bake sale table to fill my face with sugar.

Instead, I found myself saying, "I want to."

He reached down and took my hand. "Me too."

Just then, a microphone squelched and a male voice with a thick Texas accent echoed through the building.

"Ladies and gentlemen, good people of Rocky Gulch," he called out. "Welcome to the seventy-first annual Fall Four Seasons Dance. Jake has the Lone Star punch flowing, Helena and Abigail have put together a veritable feast with generous donations from the Main Street Market and the Yellow Rose Cafe, and the Longhorn Boys are ready to rock the house."

Everyone gathered in the ice house cheered as the band—the Longhorn Boys—played a little jingle.

I leaned up, closer to Ty's ear, and whispered, "I'm scared."

He laughed. Without looking away from the stage, he replied, "You probably should be."

"Now don't y'all forget to pick up some sweet treats from the bake sale table back there," the announcer said. "Not only are those the best pralines and pecan pies in five counties, but every last penny goes into the town scholarship fund."

The crowd cheered again, and I cast Ty a sideways glance. When I did, I caught sight of Genevieve's friends, the twins Ashley and Emily, standing a few feet away. They looked at Ty like he was the last praline on the table.

Guilt smacked me in the face. What was I doing, dancing and flirting with the cowboy, when I would be heading home in less than two weeks? He wasn't leaving Rocky Gulch and I wasn't staying. It wasn't fair.

"Maybe you should be dancing with someone else," I suggested.

Ty looked at me, frowning. "Like who?"

I shrugged and nodded toward the twins. When Ty turned to see, they immediately spun around and raced away.

"Ashley and Emily?" He sounded amused. "I've danced with them plenty over the years."

"I think they'd like to do more than dance with you," I blurted.

Ty turned back to me, his expression serious. "Those girls are like little sisters to me," he said. Then he stepped closer, leaned down. "And there is only one woman here that I want to dance with tonight."

My breath caught, both from his words and the intensity in his gaze. I only vaguely heard the announcer droning on in the background.

Then Ty smiled and I swore I saw the fireworks that Bud wanted me to capture on camera. I wondered if Eddie could see them from across the room.

"The only thing to do," the man with the microphone said, "is *dance!*"

With that, the band started playing and everyone around us coupled up.

Before I could react, Ty turned slipped his free hand behind my back and pulled me close-but-not-all-the-way to his body. "Now this, darling," he said, spinning me out onto the dance floor, "is going to be fun."

My dancing experience was limited to awkward slow-dances at school functions, who-cares-who's-watching girl dancing at bars and nightclubs, and that one painful waltz at my cousin Mildred's wedding. One-on-one country dancing was epically out of my comfort zone.

As we merged into the flow of dancers, I saw Eddie filming from the edge of the room. I threw him a desperate look and the rotten dirtbag had the nerve to wave.

I gave up and let Ty spin me away.

"You move well," he said a few songs later.

I pretended to be insulted. "You sound surprised."

"After the incident in the feed store," he replied with a mischievous grin, "I am."

I smacked him on the shoulder. "Isn't that rude to say?"

"Why?" He smiled, like he knew I was faking my irritation. "You said you couldn't dance."

"No, I said I *don't* dance," I argued. "Big difference."

Ty speared me with those bright blue eyes, calling me on my semantics argument without a word. "Besides," he said, "mostly I'm surprised that you're letting me lead."

"Really?" I leaned my head back to get a better look at his face.

"You're the kind of woman who likes to be in charge." He spun me in a tight turn, forcing me to hold on tighter. "You would rather lead than be led."

"True," I said, unable to argue with that fair assessment of my personality. I couldn't be good at my job if I didn't like to run things. "But when I'm out of my element, I have to let the experts take control."

And I knew, as we glided around the dance floor, weaving in and out of other couples and executing graceful turns I never thought myself capable of, that Ty was an expert dancer. Which made it no surprise when, more hours than I cared to count later, the mayor—the overzealous man with the microphone—declared us the winners.

The victory was all Ty, and from the cocky grin on his dimple face as we walked back to his truck, I knew he wasn't going to let me forget it.

"Oh shoot," Genevieve said when were almost to the cars. "I forgot my sweater."

"I'll get it," Ty offered.

"No, no," she insisted. "I'll be right back."

She gave Eddie a pointed look and she turned away.

"Um, I'll walk you," the big cameraman said. "I don't think I got a shot of the building exterior."

"You two just meet us at home," Genevieve called out as they rounded the corner back onto Main Street, leaving me and Ty alone.

"That was…" I shook my head.

"Not subtle," Ty finished.

A laugh burst out of me. "No," I agreed, "it wasn't."

It felt comfortable, joking with Ty. I felt comfortable with all of it, really. Talking to him, dancing with him, *being* with him. Despite our different backgrounds and our disparate lives, we just… clicked.

We walked the rest of the way to the truck, and when we reached it, Ty walked me around to the passenger door. I stood a little to the side while he unlocked it with the clicker.

When he reached for the handle, he stopped.

There was a tension in his body I hadn't seen before.

My heart beat faster.

"I may not agree with my sister's methods," he said, turning his body toward mine. His bright blue eyes stared into me, intense even in the faint glow of the streetlight. "But I can't argue with her intentions."

My breathing quickened as he leaned forward, closer, and his gaze dropped to my mouth.

And then our lips met and I forgot to breathe at all.

THE RIDE HOME from the dance was the longest of my life. Ty

didn't say a word. Every bump in the road rattled the entire truck—and my peace of mind.

What had that kiss meant? Was it a friendly peck? Did a brief meeting of lips mean something different in the Texas outback than it did in New York? Had I imagined it?

Why wasn't he saying something? Anything?!

By the time Ty pulled into the driveway at the house, every last one of my nerves was frayed to a frazzled end. When he cut the engine, I reached for the door handle immediately, intent on fleeing the tense atmosphere of the truck as quickly as possible.

"Cassie, wait."

Ty's words froze me in place.

He climbed out of the truck and circled around to my side.

While I waited for him to get there, to finish his thought, I noticed the sounds of the world around me. Leaves rustled in the wind, bugs chirped in the crisp night air, and somewhere a lonely coyote yipped at the moon—which was way less unsettling than the scream-barking in the morning. Funny how I'd thought this place so very quiet, too quiet, on my first night here. Now I the night came alive with sound.

The word that came to mind was *enchanting*.

"Look, Ty," I said when he opened my door, "I understand. Genevieve has been… overzealous about nudging us together. If it was a mistake, it was a mistake. I won't hold it against you."

"It wasn't," he replied, ducking his head to look at me. "It was not a mistake. I kissed you because *I* wanted to, not because Genevieve did—though lord knows I'm sure she does."

I bit back a laugh as he ran a frustrated hand over his head.

"It wasn't a mistake," he repeated. "But it complicates things."

I opened my mouth to ask why, but before I could say a word he gave me a look that told me exactly what he meant. Every argument I'd ever had with myself about why it would be a bad idea to pursue this connect with time flashed through my mind.

"I'm going back to New York," I said.

He shook his head. "And I'm not."

Talk about an insurmountable obstacle. There was more between New York City and Rocky Gulch, Texas, than just miles. They were cultural opposites in almost every way. Entirely different ways of life, different paces, different values. Farm fresh over five stars. Sunset on the porch versus Sondheim on Broadway. Horses and cattle instead of people and cars.

If not for the distance, though, it might have been... possible.

I'd had friends go through long-distance relationships. Most of them failed. The ones that didn't only survived because of frequent visits and the promise that one day soon they would be together again.

There really was no future for a life-long city girl and a diehard country boy. No, it wasn't like Ty and I were talking long-term relationship here, but it was a messy thought.

"You're right," I finally said. "It's complicated." I gave him a sad smile. "Too complicated."

I jumped down to the ground and started to walk past him.

Ty's fingers gripped my shoulder and spun me back toward the truck. His blue eyes burned with searing intensity.

"I didn't say it was *too* complicated." His smile popped his dimples. "Just… *complicated*."

"Complicated," I echoed.

"And as it happens," he said as he leaned closer, "sometimes I *like* complicated."

This time when our lips met, I was ready for it. I reached for it. I let the sensations take over. His mouth was strong, rough, and just soft enough to send shivers down my spine. His hand moved from my shoulder to my back, dragged me closer while pressing me back against the side of the seat. My arms wrapped around his neck, pulling myself up onto my toes.

His mouth left mine, tracing a line of kisses along my jaw and toward my neck.

The glare of headlights flashed over the truck as Genevieve's car pulled into the driveway behind us.

Ty and I jumped apart like guilty teenagers, flushed and panting. In the heat of the moment I'd forgotten we were still outside, that Genevieve and Eddie—with his camera always at the ready—weren't far behind. I'd been lost to the sensation.

I didn't know how to react. Were we supposed to be embarrassed? Nonchalant? What?

I looked to Ty for answers. He grinned. Winked at me. Then he took me by the hand and pulled me to his side as he swung the door shut behind us.

As we stepped into the crisp night, he drew me up close beside him.

"Well aren't you two just cute as a pair of possums in a pine tree?" Genevieve teased over the roof of her car.

Eddie moved to lift the camera to his shoulder.

"Don't you dare," I warned. "We're not filming *Who Wants to Date a Cowboy?*"

He lowered the camera back to his side, a knowing smirk on his scruffy face.

"Genevieve," Ty said with a nod that somehow only guys can manage. He gave one to Eddie too. "If y'all will excuse us."

Then, before I could protest, he headed for the house, with my hand held firmly in his. If I hadn't wanted to go with him, he wouldn't have forced me. But boy did I want to go with him.

TWELVE

PLACING my hands where Ty showed me, I grabbed the saddle and hefted it off the rack.

When he told me I was going to saddling up my ride by myself today, I'd had that initial moment of panic. A brief period of sheer terror. It only took a few calming breaths to remind myself that I could do this, that I'd been watching and helping Ty do it for over two weeks. If I hadn't learned by now how to do it myself, then I didn't deserve the cowgirl title.

Roughshod stood there calmly chewing on the carrot I had swiped from Genevieve's salad fixings last night. I walked up to her side, swung the saddle up, and managed to get it square on saddle blanket already sitting on her back on the first try.

"Nice," Ty said. "Next you need to—"

"Secure the cinch," I finished. "I remember."

Moving quickly, I buckled the loose end of the cinch beneath Roughshod's belly. I made sure it was tight enough not to roll me to the ground halfway out the door—learned that lesson the hard way. Then I loosely attached the rear since, making sure it wasn't so tight that it sent Roughshod into bucking bronco mode—another hard-learned lesson.

Several minutes later I had double-checked everything on the saddle and the bridle.

I mentally ran through the checklist Ty had taught me time and again. As far as I could remember, I'd done everything. But had I? What if I missed something important? What if something was loose or I'd left something unfastened or—

I turned to Ty, panic welling. "What did I—"

"Perfect ten," he said before I could finish asking what I'd missed.

His smile sent my panic running.

"Really?" My entire body beamed with pride. "I did every-thing right?"

Ty smiled, his eyes taking on that hooded look that I was starting to recognize… and long for. It had been two days since the Four Seasons Dance, two days since that kiss and what came after. Such a short span of time to have fallen into such a comfortable pattern with each other.

"Well let's see…" He moved closer to me, pinning me between his body and the docile mare's. He reached around one side and tested the cinch.

"Cinch is tight."

Then he leaned around the other way and traced his fingers over the leather bridle.

"Bridle is in place."

"So it's all good?" I asked.

He stood up straight and nodded.

In retrospect, I was probably just giddy with pride. But in that moment, I couldn't have stopped myself from flinging my arms around his neck and pulling his mouth to mine if a stampede of angry cattle had burst into the barn.

After a moment, he placed his hands on my hips and held me back.

I'd made myself an unspoken promise to keep our off-camera relationship as off-camera as possible. I didn't want to use this—us—to sell or promote the show. I didn't want it to be about anything other than us. Despite the fact that we were doing the very thing Bud had advised me to do, I knew that whatever was happening between me and Ty was not for prime time viewing. It wasn't even for late night, premium cable viewing.

But it was all too easy to believe we were in a bubble and the rest of the world faded away. When Eddie did his very best to remain as invisible as possible, I often found myself forgetting he was even there.

I released my hold.

"Now there's just one thing left to do," Ty said with a lazy smile.

That smile made me think of all kinds of lazy things I wanted to do with him. Things I need to *not* think about until we were off camera. "What's that?"

"Mount her."

I blinked. Several times. "Excuse me?"

"Get on the horse, Cassie," he said with a teasing wink. "Keep your mind out of the gutter, city gal."

"Oh, right." I vaguely remember that being part of my vocabulary lesson, way back on the first day. "Oh. Right!"

It took me several moments to connect what he said with the task at hand. I had saddled and bridled the horse, now it was time to reap the benefits of my hard work. It was time to ride.

Over the past two weeks, Roughshod and I had become buddies of sorts. She had gotten used to my nervous twitches and my panicked jerks to her reins. I'd gotten used to her swaying movements and tendency to stop and chop the grass if the opportunity arose.

Where I once was terrified to get in the saddle, I now looked forward to it. Life had a different perspective from the back of a horse. A perspective I was beginning to truly enjoy.

I didn't stop to wonder when riding had become a reward rather than a punishment. I pushed Ty out of my way and then reached for the saddle.

"Remember—" he started to say.

"I know," I interrupted. "Grab—" I wrapped my fingers around the saddle horn. "—set—" I lifted my foot into the dangling stirrup. "—haul and swing."

In one fluid—or at least *hopefully* fluid—motion, I lifted with my arm and leg, while flinging my other leg over the saddle to the other side. When my butt landed in saddle seat with a reassuring *thwack*, I wanted to jump up and dance. Only I was sitting on a horse who, given the right command, would take off a breakneck speed. So I settled for doing half-a-cabbage-patch with my arms.

"I did it," I sing-songed. "I did it, did it, did it."

It didn't matter how many times I pulled myself into the saddle. Every one felt like a victory.

"Come on," Ty said, handing me the reins. "Let's put this girl through her paces." He flicked a teasing glance up at me. "Roughshod needs a workout, too."

My lips pursed out in mock disgust. "You're so funny it hurts."

Then, taking the reins and—gulp—full control of the horse, I guided her out the end of the barn and into the open field.

♥

"MY BACKSIDE MIGHT NEVER RECOVER," I complained as Ty and I made our way up the porch steps after a long afternoon of riding and roping.

I looked at my hands that were rough and red from all that rope work, and I couldn't muster up a single out of regret. Or even pity.

"And my hands," I said, holding them up for display, "they worked hard today."

Ty's eyes softened as he took each of my hands in one of his. "You'll want to put some salve on them. I'll go grab Gen's special cream from the upstairs bathroom."

Then, before I had time to think, he was lifting first one hand then the other to his mouth. I shivered at the heat of his lips against the centers of my palms.

A look passed between us, and then he was inside, bounding up the stairs two at a time.

"Time for my afternoon siesta," Eddie said as he saluted and then followed Ty upstairs, heading for his guest room across the hall from mine.

I turned for the kitchen, which I had quickly learned was the heart of this house.

Genevieve stood in the doorway, an uncertain look on her pretty face.

"Look," I said, proudly holding out my rough hands like a child with a mud pie, "I roped a calf."

She glanced to my hands and then back at my face. She asked softly, "Can I talk to you for a minute?"

She seemed so serious.

"Of course."

I followed her to the kitchen table.

"I've seen the way you and my brother have been looking at each other the past few days," she said with a sad smile.

I wanted to argue with her, to deny that she had seen anything at all, but that would have been a lie. No one in a fifty-mile radius would have missed the tension simmering between me and her brother. I might not have been able to fully define it, but I couldn't deny it was there.

But hadn't she seemed to be encouraging us?

"I thought you..." I searched for the right words. "Approved?"

"I do," she said. "That's exactly my point."

"I don't follow."

"You and Ty have an obvious connection." She twisted her hands together. "I want you to encourage that."

"I... What?"

"I think you two are good for each other," she explained. "You're a good match."

I shook my head. I wasn't sure why she was saying this. Besides, what difference did it make if we were a good match? What did it matter if she approved? This thing between me and Ty couldn't last. My life, everything I'd been building, everything I had planned, was in the city. I wasn't about to give that all up for a chance on a guy and a way of life I'd only just met.

"Genevieve," I said slowly, so there was no misunderstanding, "in just over a week I'm going back to New York."

She nodded. "And I want you to take Ty with you."

To say that she stunned me silent was a massive understatement. I was completely confused. I knew that Genevieve loved her brother. That was beyond question. No one who saw them together for more than a minute could miss how much they loved each other.

So why on earth would she want me—as if I had any real control over what Ty chose to do—to drag him back to the city?

"I don't—"

"He came back because of me," she said before I could question her. "If I'd been able to run the Black Willow by myself or if I didn't love her enough so much that I couldn't bear the thought of selling her, he would have stayed in New York."

Ah, I was starting to get where she was going. "Yeah, maybe—"

"He gave up everything." Her breathing grew shallow and she looked up at the ceiling, where we could both hear Ty upstairs, rummaging through the bathroom cupboards. "His friends. His job. His *life*. It's time for him to take them back."

The guilt in her eyes was like a punch in the gut. I knew that if Ty had ever seen that, if he'd had even an inkling of an idea that she felt like this, it would have broken his heart.

"Genevieve," I said, scooting my chair around closer to hers. "Sweetie, I may not have known your brother for very long, but the one thing about which I am absolutely, one-thousand-percent certain is that he has no interest in going back to New York."

She wiped at watery eyes. "I know he says that, but—"

"No buts," I said firmly. "If anything, he's *glad* that you and the ranch drew him home."

"You really think so?"

"I know so." I placed my hand over hers. "He's happy here. You can't look at him for ten seconds without seeing that he is a man completely content with his lot in life."

She closed her eyes, head lowered, as if she was trying to process my words. Trying to make herself believe.

Boot steps echoed in the hall upstairs.

"If that's true," she said, "then please be careful."

The boot steps clattered down the stairs.

"Because if you're going back and he's not—" She looked me straight in the eye. "—then I'm going to be the one left to pick up the pieces."

"Found it," Ty called out as he appeared in the doorway.

I looked up to see him carrying a small green tin. The grin on his face was nothing short of beautiful.

Another punch in the gut.

Genevieve was right. I needed to be careful. I needed to make sure to Ty knew there was no chance of me staying in Texas. I needed to make sure I knew that too. He wasn't the only one who might get hurt in this situation, and once my career was back on track I wouldn't have time to fall to pieces.

THIRTEEN

GENEVIEVE KNOCKED on my open bedroom door Monday morning. "You ready to go to town?"

I paused for a moment, wondering just when I had started thinking of this as *my* bedroom. It was a guest room and I was a guest. Nothing more. And only for another week at that.

Rather than stop to think about why my enthusiasm for leaving Texas as soon as humanly possible had waned to going-home-in-a-week-yay levels, I asked, "Into Rocky Gulch?"

"No ma'am," she said with a huge grin. "We're heading back to Fort Worth."

She laughed when I jumped comically to my feet.

I gasped. "Really?"

I'd been wanting to visit somewhere more metropolitan than Rocky Gulch for the last few days. There were some things I needed that, sadly, the town everything store just didn't have.

"We're leaving in five," Genevieve called out as she walked away.

My brain went into overdrive. I looked down at my clothes. I was wearing my now-standard uniform of blue jeans—the lightest I'd ever worn—and a tee—this one pale green. If I changed, it would mean making everyone late. Which would mean getting to the city that much later.

I was not willing to risk it.

Besides, the last time we'd gone to town, I'd been the only one in all black. At least in this outfit I looked like I sort of belonged. I did, however, choose my black All Stars over cowboy boots. A girl has to retain some of her city roots. Besides, Genevieve's cast-off boots were fine, but they were a touch too small. After three solid weeks of wear, I had blisters-on-top-of-blisters on my toes to prove it.

I ran my fingers through my curls, swiped lip balm across my mouth, grabbed my purse, and was the first one waiting at the truck.

While I waited, I lifted my hand to shield my eyes and gazed at the rising sun. We didn't get sunrises like this in Manhattan. Oh sure, the sun rose and cast everything into an array of warm golds, soft pinks, and—occasionally—delightful lavenders. But there were always buildings. And people. And busses, and bridges, and airplanes and a million other things that served to remind you that you were not alone. That you were in a densely populated city.

Out here, nothing stood between me and the sun expect a cluster of trees and a vast expanse of grassland.

I shifted my hands to form a frame, imagining how I would film this view if I were behind the camera right now.

"You eager or something, city gal?" Ty asked as he stepped out on the porch.

I spun around, like I'd been caught sneaking into the family liquor cabinet.

My entire body inhaled the sight of him. That cocky half grin. Those jeans that fit him better than any piece of denim had a right to. The heat that lit up his eyes when he saw my reaction. If I wasn't careful, I would get too used to seeing that smile every day.

This was a temporary gig and whatever was happening between me and Ty… well, that was temporary too. It had to be.

So instead of racing over to meet him and melting into his arms—for Eddie, who walked out behind him, and the camera and, eventually, the rest of the world to see—I cocked my head to the side and said, "Don't you know it."

Genevieve was the last to arrive, running out with Babe barking at her heels.

"Sorry, sorry," she called out, waving a big envelope at the chasing dog. "I had to make a copy of the paperwork."

As we pulled away from the house, I nodded at the *Overni-teXpress* envelope she had clutched to her chest. "Important mailing?"

Her gaze dropped to the envelope and bright pink stained her cheeks.

"An application," she said, and offered nothing more.

Ty took one hand off the steering wheel and reached back to pat her on the knee. I didn't press the issue, because a girl was entitled to her secrets.

I turned and gazed out the window. As the gold-washed Texas countryside blurred by, my brain jumped forward in time. Only one week until the shooting wrapped on the *Try It*

On pilot. Only one week until I could finally escape the middle of nowhere and get back to civilization. Permanently.

Instead of the pure glee at the thought that I'd felt during my first few days in Texas, this time the prospect actually made me a little sad. Suddenly, instead of thrilling at the idea of eating up the distance between the ranch and the city, I found myself studying the countryside, wanting to take it all in, to memorize every last cow, tree, and abandoned barn on the way.

"What's on your must-do list this time, city gal?" Ty asked.

I pulled my attention away from the countryside and considered his question. "Sushi, of course."

He laughed. "Of course."

"And I want to hit up a phone store and see if I can find something that will actually work out here in the middle of nowhere." My time in Siberia might have been almost over, but I still didn't like the idea that my phone wouldn't work in every possible location.

As a producer, I couldn't control where a new project would take me. I could be right back in the middle of nowhere the week after I got back.

"Anything else?"

"If we have time to go back to Buchanan's," I said, "I'd like to get a pair of boots of my own."

Genevieve applauded. "We'll make you a cowgirl yet."

"Well I don't know about that," I said, ignoring the tingle of warmth in my chest at her words, "but my feet would like to wear something that actually fits. It's not like the work is going to get any easier over the next few days."

Ty laughed again, and I melted a little more.

"No, it's not," he said.

Between his cocky grin and Genevieve's smug look, I had a feeling I was in for a big step up in my workload on the ranch. I made a mental note to pick up a pair of work gloves, too.

"Besides," I replied, "I could totally make boots work in the city."

Eddie shifted and I sensed the camera zoom in on my face.

The moment I said the words, the mood in the truck deflated a few notches. Like no one thanked me for the reminder that our little sojourn in the country was almost over. As much as I didn't want to face the reality that I would be leaving Ty soon, I did none of us any service to pretend like it wasn't going to happen.

With a quiet contemplation filling the truck, I turned my attention back out the window. The closer we got to the city, the more traffic we met on the freeway. By the time we hit the suburbs, it was brake lights and headlights as far as I could see.

"Why is there so much traffic?" I grumbled.

"Rodeo week," Genevieve answered. "Brings both city and country folk out in droves."

"What's the matter, city gal?" Ty asked. "You starting to forget what traffic is like?"

"No," I replied. "I've never liked traffic."

That wasn't entirely true. I loved the chaos of it, the feeling that everyone was on edge and anything could happen. At any moment, the entire jam could break or we could be stuck in the same block for an hour.

I loved uncertainty—I couldn't have been a TV producer if I didn't.

But tonight, for some reason, it all annoyed me. I only wanted to get parked somewhere so I could find a new phone, buy the perfect pair of boots, and get my sushi fix for the week.

The traffic on I-20 had other ideas.

It took twice as long to get from the city line to the down-town exit as it had the first time we trekked into the city. And then, when we did, it was cars and people everywhere. Taxi drivers dove in and out of lanes, people stepped out in front of the truck without even looking, and a police barricade made us take a circular detour around the core of downtown.

In addition to being rodeo week, it was lunchtime on a gorgeous Monday, which meant every office worker in the downtown area was out on their lunch break.

Even the noise of the city was grating on my nerves. Engines and horns and shouts echoed off the buildings in an ever-growing cacophony of sound. I had to fight the urge to place my hands over my ears.

I closed my eyes and took a deep breath. The isolation of the ranch must have been getting to me. It was like a sensory deprivation chamber. A place where man-made sounds were drowned out by to natural world. Had I, in such a short time, grown more accustomed to rooster crows, soft whinnies, and the sound of the wind in the trees and grass? Was that even possible?

"I made a reservation at *Samurai Sam's* at seven," Ty said. "I'll drop you off at Buchanan's, take Gen to mail her applica-tion, and then we can all meet at the restaurant."

"Sounds good." I smiled, despite the disappointment in knowing that Ty wouldn't be there to help me pick out my boots.

"Nonsense," Genevieve said. "The *OvernightXpress* place is only a few blocks from Buchanan's. You help Cassie find her boots. Lord knows she needs more help with that than I do to drop off a package."

It took all my focus not to throw her a grateful smile. I had no clue whether she'd noticed my disappointment, but I knew that despite her reservations she was keen on seeing me and Ty together. Maybe she thought that I would eventually reconsider my return to New York. I didn't want to give her any hope that her efforts might actually work out.

I needed to start reminding everyone, including myself, that time was running out.

"That's good," I said, "because it'll be better film if Ty is there too."

She rolled her eyes at me.

I don't think either of us missed the dark look that crossed Ty's face. I wasn't wrong. It would make better television. And it would be a bad idea to keep pursuing this thing between us that could never go anywhere past the next ten days of filming.

Still, a heavy weight settled in my chest at the thought that my dismissive words might have hurt him, even a little bit.

♥

THIS TIME, walking into Buchanan's wasn't an overwhelming experience. I knew exactly what I was looking for and where to find it.

As I navigated the store, weaving through aisles and displays as Ty and Eddie trailed behind me, I realized that this time I could spot the tourists from a mile away. They always had on more makeup than sense and their clothes looked crisp, fresh, and completely clean. The true cowboys and cowgirls had a kind of… grit to them. Their hair was softer, their clothes well-worn and there was often either some current dirt or the faint stain of past dirt.

I smiled, knowing that the hoof print from when I startled Roughshod by walking behind her was still imprinted on the thigh of my jeans.

For the first time, I truly felt like a cowgirl.

"What kind of boots are you looking for?" Ty asked. "Ropers? Ostrich? Lizard?"

Ew, gross. I might not have been as much of a spoiled city girl as I had been three weeks ago, but even the idea of wearing lizard skin still made me nauseous.

"Nope," I said, marching past the designer boots with fancy patterns and colorful leathers.

I remembered Bethany telling me once about her boot shopping experience during *One Straight Guy*—she and the show's fashion expert had visited the biggest boot shop in the city, a huge warehouse-like place in the Village. Until I visited Buchanan's, I didn't think I really understood what that shopping experience had been like.

Now I knew.

As I made my way to the end of the second row of ladies boots, I spied the perfect pair. They were the same brand and style as the ones Genevieve had lent me, only instead of the tan, sueded nubuck finish, they were smooth and black.

I squatted down and found the box with my size.

"Nice choice," Ty said as he draped an elbow on the shoe rack, leaning as casually against the metal shelf as he did the wooden fence back at the ranch.

He did seem to find a way to fit in wherever he was.

"I do like the ones I've been wearing." I pulled the stuffing and the cardboard shaper out of the first boot. "But they're just a tad too small."

"And a tad too un-black?"

I looked up at him as I stuffed my left foot into the left boot. "Are you teasing me, Ty Haywood?"

"Could be," he said with a wink.

My heel slid into place. I grabbed the other boot.

"Can't give up all my city girl ways at once," I asked, "now can I?"

He smiled and shook his head as I pulled on the other boot.

"See." I held one booted foot out for inspection. "Perfect."

"Give it a walk," he said, motioning for me to take a circle around the store.

I smoothed my jeans down over the boots and then took a stroll through the store. When I got back, Ty was grinning.

"What?" I asked.

"Nothing," he said, then jerked back when I tried to smack his shoulder. "You just look mighty comfortable in those."

I shrugged and glanced down. "There's no law that says a city girl can't wear cowboy boots."

"Cow*girl* boots," he corrected. "And no, I suppose there isn't."

As I carried the box, with my well-worn sneakers tucked safely inside, to the register, I considered his words. I had become comfortable in cowboy—cow*girl*—boots. Way more comfortable than I ever imagined myself being when I first arrived in Texas.

It was good to know that I was more adaptable than I thought.

The saleswoman offered to box up the boots for me, but I wanted the glory of wearing my first pair out of the store.

I stumbled for a moment when I realized I considered these my *first* pair. Not my *only* pair.

The city streets had calmed. There were still a fair number of people navigating the sidewalks, but the car traffic had eased. There was enough space for Eddie to move around in front of us and walk backward so he could get the head-on angle, without risk of running over someone.

The pace of everything felt a little slower. A little more mellow.

No matter how quiet and calm New York got, the city never felt *mellow*. There was always a simmering energy just below the surface, a vibrancy that promised action and excitement at any moment.

Fort Worth had a different kind of energy.

"You look content," Ty observed.

"Fort Worth is growing on me," I replied.

I didn't miss the considering look he gave me, but I did ignore it.

"Did you need to stop by the drugstore?" he asked.

"No. Why?"

"Thought you might need more of those antacids you pop like candy."

"Oh. Yeah, maybe."

It took me a stunned moment of consideration to realize that maybe I didn't. I couldn't remember the last time I'd felt the need to reach for my ever-present bottle. I dug around in my purse, pulled out the bottle I'd bought the last time we were in town, and found it still more than half full.

"No, actually," I said, shoving the bottle back into my back. "I don't any."

Ty smiled at me and I had to wonder what it meant that I hadn't gone through my usual bottle-a-week.

Genevieve was already seated when we got to the restaurant. Eddie set up the tripod so the camera would catch the three of us—me, Ty, and Genevieve—throughout the meal. From his seat at the next table, he could swivel the camera to change up who was in the center of the shot.

"All set?" Ty asked his sister as we sat.

"Yes," she squealed. She was practically bouncing with energy. "It's in the mail."

I made a show of placing my napkin in my lap and opening my chopsticks. Genevieve hadn't wanted to discuss her mysterious package in the truck, so I didn't want to push the issue.

Turned out, I didn't have to.

"It's an application," she told me. "For New Amsterdam College of Music."

"NACoM? In New York?" I couldn't have been more shocked if she'd told me she was pregnant with an alien baby.

"Yes," she said, leaning forward across the table. "You gave me the courage to apply."

"*I* did?" I frowned.

"You did. In our conversation about New York.

She hesitated a fraction before saying *New York*, and I knew what she really meant was *Ty*.

"I was supposed to start at Julliard after high school," she continued, "but I deferred."

"She means her douchebag ex *made* her defer," Ty interjected.

Genevieve frowned at him. "He didn't *make* me," she argued, "but we were going to get married."

If the dark scowl on Ty's face was any clue, he wasn't going to be forgiving said douchebag ex for the *were going to* part anytime soon. Ty had a generally kind demeanor, but I wouldn't want to be on his bad side. And hurting one of his loved ones put someone clearly on the bad side.

"I'm really excited for you," I told Genevieve, trying to steer the conversation away from bad sides and douchebag exes. "What are you planning to study?".

"Voice." She blushed. "I've always wanted to be a singer."

Ty squeezed her hand across the table. "Don't let her modesty fool you. Gen's got the most beautiful voice in all of Texas."

"Don't I know it," I said. "I've heard her singing around the house. When would you start?"

"Not until the new year," she said. "I'm too late for the fall semester deadline."

"You're welcome to stay with me while you're looking for a place," I offered. "I don't have an extra bedroom, but my couch is more comfortable than most beds."

"Oh my gosh," she squealed. "That would be wonderful."

As much as I was excited for Genevieve and eager myself to get back to the city, it also made my chest a little tighter to think about leaving Texas. To think about leaving Ty.

Genevieve might have been thrilled to give city life a try, but Ty was done with that way of life. He had spent years in New York and showed no interest in going back. His roots were here, buried deep in the soil of the family ranch.

I glanced over at him, and he was focused on unfolding his napkin. Had he felt it too? That our weird connection was tightening, stretching taut over the distance that was about to come between us. With him anchored here in Texas and me straining to get back to the city, it could never work.

It would be better for both of us if I buried those feelings as deep as Ty's Texas roots.

Part of me was afraid, though, that it wouldn't be as easy as I needed it to be.

FOURTEEN

THIS TIME when I woke up, I wasn't surprised to find my room bathed in darkness. Again, the barest hint of morning glow peeked in through my window, but otherwise the world was still asleep. No birds chirping or roosters crowing. No cattle trampling the earth to get to breakfast. No horses whinnying to get theirs. No scream-barking coyote to terrify the life out of me.

No sounds of Genevieve or Ty moving around the house.

The entire world was quiet.

I, however, was wide awake.

Normally not anything close to a morning person, it seemed that my mind and body were eager to get up and running this morning. Maybe it was the knowledge that filming would wrap soon and I would be leaving this beautiful place forever.

I laid still for as long as I could bear, absorbing the way the tendrils of sun angled across the cracked ceiling of my room, the fresh, damp smell of the morning air that washed in my open window on a gentle breeze. I tried to memorize the details, wishing I had a camera within reach but forcing myself to commit them to memory instead.

But after a few minutes I grew antsy. Itching to start the day.

The fact that I actually wanted to get up and moving should have been a sign of the apocalypse. Instead of burying my head back under the pillows, I swung myself out of bed and got dressed quickly. I grabbed my new boots and tread carefully down the stairs, not wanting to wake anyone up with my clomping.

I was eager to break them in.

Babe met me at the base of the stairs.

"Hey girl." I patted her on the head on my way across the hall.

The smell of coffee wafted out of the kitchen. I groaned with relief.

I dashed in to pour myself a cup that had been set to auto-brew at ungodly-o-clock in the morning. As I turned to leave, I saw a large, shadowy figure filling the kitchen door.

Not Babe.

"Morning, city gal." Ty's voice was gruff with sleep.

I smiled even though he probably couldn't see it in the almost dark. "Morning, cowboy."

He walked into the kitchen. I handed him my untouched mug of coffee and then poured myself another.

"You ready to work?" he asked.

I nodded. "Yep. Let's break in these boots."

We didn't say another word. I quickly pulled on my boots and we slipped out the back door, our coffee and our breath steaming in the crisp morning air.

"This is my favorite time of day," he said as we made our way to the barn. "Everything is so peaceful. Quiet."

"I always hated the quiet," I confessed.

"Past tense?" he asked.

He didn't miss much. "Maybe," I said. "I've gotten kind of used to it. Learned to enjoy the stillness. I guess I never had the chance to try it out for more than a few days at a time before."

"That's the city for you."

"Yeah," I agreed as Ty held open the barn door for me, "but it was more than that. I was always rushing from one project to the next, one production to the next. Always in a hurry."

"Not much call for hurry out here."

"No, it's a whole different rhythm." I walked into the feed room and started lining up the morning feed supplies. "More cyclical. The repetitive nature of the pattern is soothing. Get up. Feed the horses. Clean the stalls. Check the fence line. It's… reassuring."

Ty moved behind me, filling the containers with measured amounts of grain. "Now you see why I can't go back," he said. "I don't want to. I won't let myself lose this connection to the natural rhythm of things again. The city is the opposite of this."

"I know," I said quietly.

There was no ultimatum or censure in his statement, but it was a clear dividing line. He would be staying here, with the slower pace of the ranch and country life. We both knew I wouldn't, that I had to return to the city. I might have been growing more used to the country, might have even been growing to enjoy it. New York was not the all-powerful magnet it had been when I arrived in Texas a few short weeks ago, but it was still my home. Just because I found things to love about Texas didn't mean I wanted to move there. Didn't mean I could even seriously consider it.

The heaviness in the air was stifling.

"It's so fresh this morning," I said, more brightly than I felt.

"Fall is speeding by," Ty replied, seemingly just as happy to ignore the tense moment between us. "Winter won't be far behind."

And then there were no more words, there was only the work. The sun had crested the horizon before I even realized that Eddie was nowhere in sight. I had been doing the work… just because.

I wondered what that meant.

♥

"OH SHOOT," Genevieve cursed. "We're out of yeast."

Her apron was covered with flour and she had been busy baking and cooking all night. I kept offering to help, but she insisted that it was a form of therapy. She was going to be a worried mess until she heard back about her application. Baking helped her keep calm.

Still, I stayed in the kitchen, casually reviewing footage on my laptop and ready to leap to her aid at any moment.

Eddie was trying out a few experimental shots with the camera. His latest appeared to be shooting through a jar of blue-tinted water.

Ty walked up behind Genevieve and rubbed her shoulders. "You need some before tomorrow? I'm picking up the new saddle in the morning."

She turned and gave him a pleading look. "I need some tonight, or we won't have biscuits at breakfast."

Ty groaned, but I could tell it was a fake groan.

"You know I love your biscuits," he said. "I'll go into town."

"I'll go with you," she said. "You'll never pick out the right kind."

"You kids have fun," I called out as the headed for the door. "Eddie and I will hold down the fort."

Genevieve blew me a kiss and then they were gone.

The moment they were out of the house, Eddie set the camera down—still rolling, but down. "Did you call Bud back yet?"

I shook my head. "I haven't had time."

Bud had called while I was out working. Genevieve took the message, which said he wanted me to call him back as soon as possible. Since I didn't know whether it would be good news or bad, I hadn't wanted to call in front of the Haywoods. Eddie and I were used to the mercurial temperaments of studio heads. They were not.

I pulled my new flip-phone out and tried to find the call app. I'd had the thing for days and still hadn't managed to make a single call. Apparently it was too old school for me to operate. It had signal… I just couldn't use it.

"I can work a smartphone," I complained, "but not a dumb one. What does that say about me?"

"Here," Eddie said, taking it from my hand, "I'll dial."

He studied the phone, which apparently confused him too. "What the—" He scowled and shook his head. "Oh, here it is."

The sound of a ringing phone filled the room.

"Crap, looks like it's on speaker—"

"Bud Gorman's office," a tired voice said.

I held a finger up to Eddie, indicating he should be silent. Bud was not a fan of conference calls. I didn't want to give him any reason to be irritated.

"Hi Marian, it's Cassie Bishop," I said cheerfully. "I'm calling Mr. Gorman back. Is he in?"

"Hold please."

Elevator music filled the room.

I shoved the phone at Eddie. "Fix it!"

He fumbled with it, tapping and punching buttons to no avail. "I can't," he said, "it's fro—"

The elevator music cut off abruptly.

"Bishop," Bud's voice boomed through the phone, "it's about damn time."

"Hi Bud," I said, snatching the phone back from Eddie. "Sorry, it's been a busy day and I couldn't get away."

I shot my cameraman a glare.

"Hate to be the bearer of bad news," he said, "but the focus group data isn't good."

I exchanged a deflated look with Eddie. Bad focus group data was the kiss of death. No matter how much any or all of the studio executives loved a project, if it fell flat with the target audience it was all but canned.

"But I thought things were looking better," I argued. "After the last round—"

"It's not your fault," Bud interrupted. "You did a terrific job playing up the romance angle like I asked. Female viewers eighteen to thirty-five gave you and the cowboy high marks. They rated you, what was that term..." I could hear him shuffling papers. "Oh yes, *Fifty Shades of the Wild West*. Couldn't have asked for more."

That only made me feel worse. I'd been doing my best to keep the chemistry between me and Ty off-screen. I hadn't wanted it to be part of the show. Clearly I'd failed. Just as clearly as I'd failed with the overall production.

I started to hang my head, but Eddie made some kind of choking sound. I looked up, ready to glare at him again, until I saw his eyes were bugged out and staring at something over my shoulder. The hair on the back of my next tingled and I knew exactly what I was going to see when I turned around.

The look on Ty's face was disturbingly blank. No hint of confusion or anger or betrayal. Just… nothing.

He couldn't have heard that. My luck was bad, my karma clearly running in the red, but even I wasn't so unlucky that Ty would have overhead Bud saying that I'd done a good job basically faking our romance for the camera.

Oh yes, my luck was that bad.

"Forgot our reusable bags," he said, snatching the collection from the hook just inside the door. "Gotta do our part to save the planet."

"Ty, I—"

But he was gone, the front door slamming behind him.

"Bishop!" Bud barked. "Am I on speakerphone?"

I slumped onto the table.

"No sir," I lied.

"Good," he said, "because you need to hear this first."

I sank deeper, mumbling, "Hear what?" as I covered my head with my hands.

"You're getting one last chance," Bud said. "The board is

letting you finish the pilot shoot, but if things don't improve…"

He didn't finish the threat. He didn't have to. If the last few days of filming didn't turn things around, the show was going to be canned. And I was going to be hunting for a new job.

Could things get any worse?

FIFTEEN

TY AND GENEVIEVE didn't get back until late. And when the rumble of the truck roared up the road, I braced myself for a confrontation—for an opportunity to explain the situation—that never came. Genevieve walked through the door alone.

She didn't say where Ty had gone, just dove back into preparations for the next morning's breakfast. Happily humming a tune as if nothing had happened.

Ty must not have told her what he overheard.

The look on his face after he heard Bud's words haunted me. All the spark, all the energy that seemed to keep him always smiling, always happy, had been extinguished. I hated knowing that I had, in some small—or not so small—part contributed to that loss.

I didn't want to go to bed without explaining things to him.

I fell asleep at the kitchen table.

When I woke up at some point in the middle of the night with a painful crick in my neck, I dragged myself upstairs and spent an hour staring at the cracked ceiling above my bed. Not even the coyote was scream-barking. Dark silence surrounded me, like the entire world had shunned me for hurting Ty.

I understood. I would shun me too.

At least I knew that in morning I would be able to explain things. To tell him that, despite what Bud said, I hadn't faked anything. I hadn't been able to, and I wouldn't have even if I could. I only hoped that he would believe me.

I was exhausted, emotionally and physically, but sleep was having none of it. My mind kept racing, playing through Bud's words, over and over. The misunderstanding between me and Ty was bad enough—at least I would be able to explain that and hope that he believed me. I had faith that he would. But the threat that not even the now-sizzling attraction between me and Ty could save the show from the dead project bin was a bigger blow.

I had spent the last three and a half weeks putting my everything into making this pilot work. I put my life on hold, shed my city slicker attitude, and threw myself headfirst into the cowgirl life. If I was being honest with myself, I enjoyed it far more than I ever imagined I could.

Still, it had been a means to an end. The direct path back to my career. No other reason could have ever tempted me into the Texas outback.

What if it had all been for nothing?

For the first time in days, I rolled over and reached for the bottle of antacids on my nightstand. The fear that my time at the Black Willow had been wasted brought all of my stress back into my stomach.

I had just downed a pair of cherry chewables when someone knocked on my door.

Ty, my mind gasped.

Somehow, in the course of my worrying and mental meandering, the sun had risen and filled my room with the glow of mid-morning.

Whether he had come for a confrontation or an explanation or just to tell me it was time to get to work, I leaped out of bed, my heart pounding in anticipation of seeing him on the other side. But when I pulled open the door, Genevieve stood there with a panicked look on her face.

My breath caught in my throat. "Ty?"

"He left before dawn," she said, her voice shaking. "Said he heard that coyote howling closer to the house. He rode out to make sure our herds were safe."

I forced myself to breathe.

"I'm sure he's fine," I insisted, though I had nothing more than hope and faith to base my claim on. He just had to be.

"He was just going to ride out and right back. Didn't want to take his truck or the ATV and disturb the neighbors." She bit her lip. "Cassie, I'm worried."

"What about Victor and Jesse?" I asked. "Can they go look for him?"

"They took a load to the stockyards yesterday," Genevieve said. "They won't be back until tomorrow."

"Okay then." I left her in the doorway and grabbed yesterday's jeans off the floor. I didn't hesitate as I told her, "*We'll* go find him."

Seconds later, I was hopping into my boots as we headed down the hall.

Babe bounded after us, but at the door Genevieve made her stay. She would only add another variable into a stressful situation.

My mind threatened to dissolve into panic, but I refused to

let that happen. Freaking out was not going to help us find Ty. I had to keep my clear-thinking producer hat on.

We ran to the barn. Genevieve got LucyLoo out of her stall while I haltered Roughshod. My brain went on autopilot, taking me through everything that Ty had taught me over the past few weeks. In less time than I would have believed possible, Genevieve had settled into the saddle on LucyLoo and I was climbing up onto Roughshod.

Genevieve smiled at me through her fear. "You're a natural, Cassie Bishop."

"I've had a good teacher." I pulled up next to her as we guided the horses out into the pasture. "Which way did he go?"

"He said he was going to check down by the old spring," she said. "Daddy cleared away a den down there when we were little. Ty always worries that a new pack will move in."

I nodded and nudged Roughshod into a trot.

As the immediate concern of getting the horses outfitted over, my clear-thinking faded a bit and worry took its place. Riding was a dangerous act, and riding out alone in the pre-dawn darkness had to be borderline stupid. Ty was experienced and capable, but even he couldn't handle every situation. There could have been a snake or a rabbit or another critter that startled his big, brawny gelding, Demonite. They could have had a run in with the coyote.

If I ever met that scream-barking moron coyote his neck and my hands were going to have a conversation.

But for every possible worst-case scenario that popped up, I forced myself to shove it back down. Not only would worrying *not* help or change the situation, but I had to believe that Ty was fine. I had to believe in him enough to think that he was able to take care of himself. He was a responsible, experienced rider.

Another tiny kernel of fear poked at the back of my consciousness, wondering if maybe, somehow, whatever happened to Ty this morning has something to do with the phone call he heard last night.

What if he rode angry or distracted and that's why something happened to him? He had told me, time and again, that horses responded to human emotion. What if Demonite had reacted badly to Ty's feelings as they rode out together? What if—

No, I would not let myself go down that path.

Ty was fine. He had to be.

♥

"OH THANK GOD," Genevieve cried out.

I nudged Roughshod into motion, racing after Genevieve as she broke into a gallop toward the cluster of trees around the spring. As I drew closer, I saw the bright red of the plaid shirt Ty had worn yesterday. He must have pulled it on in his rush to get out the door.

He sat on the edge of a big rock, his right leg stretched out straight in front of him and a pained look on his face.

I was so relieved to see him, to see that he was okay, that I almost cried.

Genevieve leaped to the ground before LucyLoo fully stopped, jumping into a run toward her brother.

"I was scared to death," she cried. "What the hell happened?"

"Demonite got spooked and threw me."

"He didn't come back to the barn." She skidded to stop, and practically dove onto the rock next to him, throwing her arms around his neck.

"You know Dem," Ty said through a wince, "he loves to stop and talk to the ladies. Never had the heart to tell him he's a gelding."

"Are you okay?" I asked, climbing down as soon as Roughshod stopped—I wasn't anywhere near confident enough in my novice riding skills to take a running dismount.

Ty turned to look at me, and I braced myself for anger or dismissal, some kind of reaction based on the overheard phone call. I wouldn't have blamed him. But instead, he gave me a sheepish smile.

"I'm fine," he insisted. "Twisted my knee in the fall. Aggravated the old war wound."

"War wound?" I didn't even know Ty had served.

"He means football," Genevieve quickly explained. "In Texas, every boy serves time in the pigskin forces."

I laughed with relief. "Will you be okay?"

He nodded. "Just need some quality time with an ice pack and a bandage wrap."

"Can you walk?" she asked her brother.

"If I could," he replied with a self-effacing smile, "I wouldn't still be sitting here on this rock."

"LucyLoo is too small to carry the extra weight." She turned to me. "He'll have to ride back on Roughshod."

"Okay," I said. "What do I have to do?"

"If this lummox can get up on this boulder," she said, taking Roughshod's reins from me and leading her over to the rock, "then maybe he can mount the horse without too much help."

Even before his sister had finished, Ty was up on his good leg, maneuvering himself to a standing position. He braced his hands on the saddle. "I'll need a leg up."

"I'll hold Roughshod in place," Genevieve instructed. "Cassie, you go help him."

Somehow, between the three of us and Roughshod—steady, patience beast that she was—we managed to get Ty up and in the saddle.

"I'll meet you all back at the barn," I said, turning to jump down from the boulder.

It had to be at least a twenty-minute trek, but it was no less than I deserved. And I would give me a little more time with the country. My time was running out and I wouldn't begrudge the long walk home.

"Not so fast," Ty said, his strong hand wrapping around my shoulder before I could get down off the rock. "You're riding behind me."

My gaze flashed to Genevieve. She shrugged innocently and then pulled herself up onto LucyLoo. "I'll take the lead," she said, her tone light. "To make sure there are no more critters to spook the horses."

"Come on, city gal," Ty said, extending his hand down to me. "You need to learn how to ride double. Consider it part of your test."

I let him help me up and I settled into place behind him.

"You'll have to hold tight." He took my hand and pulled it forward, around his waist. "There's not much to keep you on the horse back there."

As he nudged Roughshod into motion, I squeezed. Eventually, the hypnotizing motion, the swaying back and forth combined the relief at finding Ty safe and sound, lulled me into a blissful state of half sleep half dream. My entire body relaxed and I leaned forward to rest my cheek against his back.

But even the hypnotic movement of Roughshod's gentle walk couldn't keep the memory of last night's phone call away for long. I needed to explain things.

"Ty, about last night —"

He stiffened immediately, his entire body tensing.

"It's fine," he said.

"No, Ty," I said. "It's not fine. I know it sounded bad. What Bud said, it sounded… horrible."

He didn't reply, but he didn't stop me either, so I took that as a good sign. Or at least as permission to continue.

"Yes, Bud asked me to play up the, um—" How could I say that without sounding even worse than it already was? "To play up the… chemistry between us. For the cameras."

He remained silent, so I continued.

"The focus groups weren't loving the show," I continued, "and he thought that adding a romance angle would make it more appealing."

"Did it?" he asked, his voice stiff.

It didn't, but I didn't want to break the news to him that the show was on the verge of cancellation before we'd even finished filming. Not yet.

"I didn't do it," I said, pretending to mishear his question. "I didn't play up anything between us." Then realized I didn't want even a half-lie between us. "Actually, I did try. Once. It was a disaster."

He was silent for several seconds, and then asked, "At the feed store?"

I closed my eyes and burrowed my face against his back. I replied with a muffled, "Yes."

He actually laughed out loud. The rumble in his chest vibrated against my cheek and I couldn't help but laugh too.

"That was…" He laughed again. "Unusual."

"It was an epic failure," I corrected. "Which was partly why I didn't try again."

He asked softly, "What was the other part?"

"I couldn't…" I started, feeling awkward. "It felt wrong to exploit something as important as—" I almost said love, but that felt like way too big a word for this moment. Too big and not big enough. "As romantic feelings for the sake of the show."

We rode in silence for a few moments as I thought back over the past three and a half weeks. I'd almost said the word love, almost made a confession I wasn't sure I would ever be ready to make. But whether or not I gave it that four-letter label didn't change my feelings for Ty. I cared about him. I felt that thing that connected my heart to his. He needed to know that.

"Everything that happened between us," I said quietly, "it was all real."

His strong hand closed over mine where they rested just above his belt buckle. Nothing more than that—no words, no reassurances or promises. Just the simple gesture of his hand on mine, and I knew he understood. I knew he felt it too.

After several more beats of silence, he finally asked, "What exactly was that spectacle in the feed store?"

I snorted. "The stumble-catch."

"Stumble-catch?" he echoed.

"Well, a failed one anyway."

"Do I even want to know?"

I shook my head. "Probably not."

I thought he would leave it at that, but he said, "Tell me anyway."

I smiled as I explained about Isobel and her guy-catching tactics.

"One night, senior year, we went down to this awful bar called the Packing House in Tribeca," I told him. "She got twenty phone numbers in one night. It was a world record or something."

Ty twisted in the saddle. "I've been to the Packing House."

"Really?"

My mind reeled with the collision of my two worlds. All this time in Texas, even knowing that Ty had lived in New York for several years, I never really connected that with *my* New York. It was like Ty in New York was in a bubble that couldn't possibly have intersected with my world.

But knowing that he had gone to the same bar that I had gone to was mind-boggling. We might have even been there at the same time.

I squeezed myself a little closer against his back.

What if we had met that night? What if our worlds had collided on *my* turf, back in the city, instead of on his out here in the country? Would I have given him a second look? Would he have given me one?

I'd been a college senior, and probably acting like an ass, so he likely wouldn't have given me even a first thought. But I couldn't imagine seeing him across the crowded bar and *not* taking notice. I couldn't imagine not needing to meet him and talk to him.

"I would have noticed you," Ty said quietly.

"Really?" I asked, surprised that he was answering my unspoken question.

"Absolutely," he said, his tone teasing. "All those curls? I couldn't have missed that."

I smacked him on the shoulder, but there was a smile on my face as I leaned back into his back. *I would have noticed you too, Ty,* I said the words silently. *I would have noticed you too.*

SIXTEEN

TY WAS ALREADY in the barn the next morning when I woke up. I'd been plagued by dreams of horses in the Packing House and nightmares of Ty drowning in the Jackie O Reservoir in Central Park, so for the first time in weeks I'd slept through sunrise. Finding the house empty, I grabbed a freshly-baked muffin from the kitchen and then hurried out to the barn.

"You ready for your final test, cowgirl?" Ty asked.

Eddie swung the camera at me.

Babe lunged for me, but I sidestepped out of her way.

"Absolutely." I forced a grin on my face.

Maybe that was why I'd overslept.

The final test, I knew, was an overnight trail ride. We would pack up the horses with food and camping gear, trek out to an isolated location—which, as far as I could tell, meant pretty much the entire ranch was up for grabs—and spend the night sleeping under the stars. I'd been both dreaming of the adventure and dreading it. I looked forward to the challenge, to be able to put everything I'd learned from Ty to the test and prove myself as, if not an actual true cowgirl, at least cowgirl-worthy.

On the other hand, I dreaded having to spend the night outdoors. In case previous observations hadn't made it clear, I wasn't the woodsy, camping type. In fact, the only two times I'd ever actually slept under the sky were both in college.

Once when a group of friends and I decided to camp out for opening night tickets for some hugely anticipated movie that I couldn't even remember the title of anymore. I'd fallen asleep leaning against the brick wall outside the box office.

The other time I'd gotten locked out of my dorm at three in the morning—long story—and had been either too drunk or too embarrassed to wake someone up to let me in.

The fact that I was planning to spend a legitimate night camping in the wilderness was more than a little dread-inducing, but that wasn't the only reason I was not looking forward to the final test. The final test meant the final days of shooting. My final days in Texas.

Less than a month ago, I couldn't have imagined being sad to say farewell to the Lone Star State. I had been nothing but eager to get in, get the pilot shot and wrapped, and get back to the real world.

Now, I had to admit, I was probably going to miss this place. I was dragging my feet because I wanted to enjoy every last moment I had in this foreign world that had started to feel all too familiar.

And, of course, I was going to miss Ty.

"All right then," he said, right as that thought brushed through my mind. He held out a halter. "Let's get started."

The key to the test was that I wouldn't be given any assistance, any instruction. I had to halter, saddle, and bridle

Roughshod all by myself. I had to attach the saddlebags and tie on my bedroll. I had to mount on my own and get on my way... all without even a hint of help from Ty or Genevieve.

The test wasn't graded. I wouldn't be punished if I failed or rewarded if I won. But still, I wanted to succeed. I wanted to prove that I had been able to overcome one of the most challenging things I'd ever faced.

I wanted to prove to myself that the little niggle of doubt at the back of my mind that I wasn't only a city girl by choice but also by necessity, was unfounded. I could cut it as a cowgirl, as a country girl if I needed to.

You never knew when a zombie apocalypse might wipe out urban life. If that day ever came, I would be prepared to survive in the rural world.

Fine, riding a horse probably wouldn't be helpful in the zombie apocalypse. But knowing I could handle any situation that headed my way—not just typical city girl ones—would be a huge sense of achievement.

Ty and Genevieve made themselves scarce, leading their horses outside while I began my work. They didn't want to risk jumping in to help me if I got stuck. It would defeat the purpose of the test if I had a safety net the entire time. I needed to be literally on my own.

"You can do this, Cassie."

I turned, startled by Eddie's words. Since shooting started, he'd remained virtually silent during filming. It was a cameraman's job to keep himself and his presence out of the final product. The viewer should never once stop to think about the person standing behind the lens.

I smiled at him, grateful for the support. "Thanks."

Then he moved the camera to his shoulder and all personal interaction was off.

I approached every step slowly and methodically. Over the past three and a half weeks I had done any and all of these steps countless times. They should have been almost second nature by now.

But I didn't always do them all at once. And never without Ty standing over my shoulder.

I drew in a deep breath through my nose. Instead of being grossed out by the dust and animal smell, I was calm. The rich earthy scent of the dirt beneath my feet, the eager whinnies and nickers of the horses wondering if they were going to be next. The underlying certainty that I could do this. I knew I could.

Roughshod was unusually patient as I went through the steps. First I put on her tack, making sure everything went on in the right order. Then I started packing on the extra gear for the overnight. I even stopped a couple of times to give her a treat or just to nuzzle her soft face.

It was hard to imagine that, less than a month ago, I'd never even met a horse. I'd been terrified of her. Now we were… friends.

"How's that, girl?" I mused when I thought I was done.

Self-doubt kicked in and I went back over the checklist again, step by step. And again. And one more time, just to make sure.

When I could face the prospect of quadruple-checking my work one more time, I deemed myself done.

I turned to face Eddie, to face the camera, with a huge grin on my face. "I think I did it."

I said it to the camera, to the thousands or hundreds of

thousands of viewers who might one day see the show—if we managed to get greenlit in the end.

I said to Eddie, who smiled from behind the lens.

I said it to the distorted reflection of myself, the new, self-reliant, not-so-terrified-of-the-country-anymore city girl who just might have found her cowgirl vibe.

All that was left was to mount up and join the Haywoods outside. Piece of cake.

When Roughshod and I emerged into the morning sun, I was met by a round of applause. Ty and Genevieve looked as proud of me as I was of myself.

"You ready to head out, city gal?" he asked.

I smiled. "Yee-haw."

I NEVER REALIZED how hilly the ranch lands got in the west. We rode for what felt like ever, first across flat planes and then up into tree- and bush-covered hills. With Ty in the lead, I followed close behind, with Eddie and his camera after me and Genevieve bringing up the rear. We wove along a barely visible path, up into a canyon.

Finally, we crested the hill.

"Oh wow," I exclaimed as Roughshod climbed up next to Ty and Demonite.

I hadn't realized how much we were climbing. From up here, I had an unobstructed view for miles around. Rich green hills off to the southwest. Dry dusty planes to the east.

"Best views in the county," Genevieve said as she pulled LucyLoo to a stop next to me. "Daddy always said this very spot was why Great-granddaddy Haywood settled here instead of pushing on west."

"It's…" I shook my head, trying to take in and comprehend all the natural beauty around me. I could only come up with one word to describe the scene. "Breathtaking."

New York had its own beauty. The geometric shapes of buildings that cut across the skyline. The contrast of glinting glass, rusting steel, and centuries-old stone. The flow of traffic on the FDR, the flow of pedestrians in Times Square. Man-made echoes of the trees, mountains, and rivers created by nature.

For the first time, I realized that the echoes couldn't compare with the real thing. Nature took beauty to the next level.

Ty jumped down off his horse without so much as a wince. Clearly the ice pack and the bandage had taken care of his twisted knee. He didn't even have a limp.

"This is where we bed down for the night."

He reached up and started untying the bundle from the back of his saddle.

"I'll hunt up some firewood," Genevieve said, climbing to the ground. "Eddie, why don't you join me."

He looked at me, asking permission maybe. He'd handled all the shooting decisions for the up until now. Why would he suddenly ask permission?

I shrugged. "You could use some setting footage."

He nodded and followed after Genevieve as she headed off into the brush.

I crossed the small clearing that would be our campground and took in the landscape of the rocky north.

"This spot is amazing," I said to Ty when we were alone. "I

had no idea there was an overlook like this on your property. You could charge money."

Ty dropped his bundle on the ground and then knelt to unroll it. "Wait until you see sunset."

I could already imagine.

No sense staring off into the horizon while there was work to be done. I started unpacking Roughshod's gear, untying the bedroll and camping supplies. I wasn't sure how things would be laid out—there was a fire pit full of ash, but I didn't know if the bedrolls should be near that, or at a distance, or where the other gear should be set up—so I just started stacking stuff neatly in a pile.

Ty and I were quietly working away when a shriek echoed through the air.

We looked at each other.

"That wasn't Gen," Ty said.

My eyes widened. "It must have been Eddie."

We both jumped to our feet and raced off in the direction the other pair had headed. About fifty feet into the brush beyond the clearing, we met them on their way back. Eddie had his left arm slung over Genevieve's shoulder, the camera still settled on his right. They were moving forward at a painfully slow pace, Eddie limp-hopping with every step.

"What happened?" Ty demanded.

Eddie cast a nervous look at Genevieve.

She clenched her jaw.

"Stepped on a rock wrong," he said. "Twisted my ankle."

I hurried forward and took the camera from him, while Ty took Genevieve's place holding the big guy upright and helping him move faster. I returned ahead of our little parade and set the camera safely out of the way.

"Let's get you settled on a bedroll," Ty was saying as they emerged into the clearing. "We need to get your ankle elevated."

Eddie glanced at Genevieve again.

She gave him an insistent look.

"Actually," Eddie said, "I think I need to go back. To the house. I have a low pain tolerance. If I don't down some aspirin soon I'm going to be unbearable."

"No problem," Ty said. He nodded at me. "There are painkillers in the first aid kit."

"Um, actually…" Genevieve looked at the ground. "I think the first aid kit got left behind."

Ty said, "I put it in your saddlebag."

"I think I took it out."

"Why?"

"I had to repack them," she replied. "To fit in the bug spray."

There was something awkward in the way she spoke, the way she explained the situation.

The strange looks between Eddie and Genevieve were starting to make sense. I walked over to LucyLoo's saddlebags and searched each one thoroughly, but I already knew I wouldn't find a first aid kit in either one. Then I searched the rest of the saddlebags. Eight compartments in all.

"Nothing," I said, turning around and giving Genevieve a skeptical look.

She didn't meet my gaze.

Ty sighed. "All right. Someone hold the big guy up while I repack the gear."

"Oh no," Genevieve said, rushing forward. "This shouldn't ruin Cassie's big night. I'll take Eddie back to the house and get him taken care of." She gestured at me and Ty. "You two stay out here and finish the shoot."

Eddie nodded. "There's a tripod strapped to the back of my saddle. Just set up the camera for a fixed shot. We'll be able to make it look good in edits."

A few minutes later, Genevieve and LucyLoo were leading Eddie and his horse back down the hill.

Ty walked up next to me as we watched them disappear.

"Did you notice," he asked, "that Eddie had no trouble getting himself back on that horse?"

I sighed. "I did notice that."

"They were in an awful hurry to get back down the hill."

"They were."

He just shook his head and went back to work getting the camp set up. I made sure the camera was set up with a wide shot and then went back to my own unpacking, following his lead as he laid out his bedroll, set out the cooking gear, and got the horses settled for the night.

A few hours later, we had cooked and eaten our very typical trail meal of skillet cornbread, spit-roasted chicken, and baked beans. I had washed the dishes with a bucket of water Ty fetched from a nearby spring and then he dried and put them away. While I moved the camera into a new position that would capture the glorious sunset, Ty made some version of coffee that looked more like sludge but tasted of delicious caffeine.

I settled onto a rock with a great view of the sunset, and a few seconds later Ty joined me.

We sat for several minutes, silently watching the sun dip into the horizon as we drank our sludge.

"Do you ever miss it?" I asked.

He understood what I meant. "Can't say never," he replied. "I had good times in New York. Over the years I've thought about going back more than once."

I drew in a breath. "Will you?"

He was silent so long I turned away from the sunset to look at him.

"No," he finally answered. "Not for more than a visit."

I nodded and turned back to face the sun. That was the crux of everything, wasn't it? Ty wouldn't go back. I couldn't stay.

The romance of the moment was almost too powerful, and I had to fight the urge to reach out and take his hand. But that way lay heartache. This was my final test. Tomorrow morning we would film the last shots, and by tomorrow afternoon Eddie and I would be back in our rented SUV and headed for the airport.

What was the point in making that goodbye even harder?

Ty's hand closed over mine.

When I looked up, he turned to face me. In the fading orange light I saw in his eyes the same emotions I battled.

"Cassie—"

I held up my hand, silencing him, and then jumped to my feet. A moment later I had shut off the camera and returned to our romantic rock.

"I know," I said, no needing him to say the words.

We leaned into each other. Our lips met and I was lost.

SEVENTEEN

"DO YOU WANT TO SAY IT?" I asked Eddie.

He leaned out from behind the camera. "Can I?"

His scruffy face broke into a huge grin when I nodded. As the senior—aka *only*—producer, it was my job, my *right* to say it. But Eddie had done so much more work than I had on the production side of this pilot that he'd more than earned.

He turned the camera around to face himself.

"Hi America," he said into his own lens. "I'm Eddie Monroe, trusty cameraman and jack-of-all-trades for *Try It On*. We've just finished filming the pilot episode." He flicked his gaze briefly at me and then back at the lens. "As they say in the movies: that's a wrap."

He held the shot for a few seconds and then reached up and punched the record button. The camera's red light dimmed to black.

"Finally!" Eddie shouted, his voice echoing down the barn aisle.

All around us, the horses looked up and peered out their stalls to see what the commotion was.

"So that's it?" Genevieve asked. "You're all done filming?"

"We are," I said.

After the night out on the trail, Ty and I rode back in this morning. Eddie met us at the barn—his ankle *miraculously* healed—and we filmed the final segment. I'd put Roughshod's tack away, brushed her down, and gave her a few treats before putting her back in her stall.

"Not that I don't love each and every one of you like my own mother," Eddie said, the camera hanging at his side like an extra appendage, "but I cannot wait to get the heck out of this state."

"If your flight is at eight," Ty said, "you should probably be on the road no later than two."

Two o'clock? I pulled out my phone and checked the time. It was already twelve-thirty. Only ninety minutes until I left the Black Willow. Forever.

"You'd better get packing," I told Eddie. If I focused on him, maybe I could keep the tide of emotion that was hovering in my chest from spilling out. "With everything you brought and bought, we'll be lucky to get out of here before dark."

Eddie blew me an exaggerated kiss. "Love you."

As he turned and headed for the house, I scanned my gaze over Ty—who was wholly occupied with something on Daisy-Day's stall door—and Genevieve. The sad look in her eyes was enough to make the tears fall.

"I'd better get packing too," I said.

When neither of them said anything—although what had I really expected them to say?—I turned and followed Eddie up the dirt path.

The end of every shoot was like a breakup. No matter how much you loved or hated the show along the way, it was still a major investment of time, emotion, and creative energy. A period of intense interaction with the cast and crew. Whenever something like that ended it was bound to be a bittersweet moment.

But I had never felt as empty and bereft as I did now, as I put one boot in front of the other and carried myself back to the house. I was finally returning to my beloved city, and yet I had the strangest urge…not to.

It must have been the confusion of being both behind the lens and on the screen. Dividing my attentions, dividing my efforts must have caused a strain on my brain that allowed the thought of staying in Texas to even form. As a cast member, I had to invest myself fully into the role of wannabe cowgirl in order to convince the audience, especially the focus groups, that the dream was real. Maybe I was a better actress than I thought. Maybe I had even convinced myself.

Once I had put some distance between myself and the ranch, the illusion would fade to black and I'd be back to my old city-bound self. I had to believe that.

As much as I'd teased Eddie about the sheer volume of stuff he had to pack, I'd forgotten about my own acquisitions. Besides my boots—which I would have to wear on the airplane, because there was no way they would fit with every-thing else I needed to pack in my carry-on—and my other purchases from Buchanan's, there was the trio of bandana bow barrettes Sue-Anne had made for me, the package of home-made beef jerky from Philly, and Genevieve had insisted I take any of the borrowed clothes that I wanted. While I definitely didn't need to take her entire wardrobe, I couldn't resist taking a few key pieces.

After much deliberation, I settled on two pairs of jeans—it

would take half a lifetime of city work to break new ones in that well—and the blue and gray plaid shirt I wore the first day I had shed my all-black uniform. That filled my suitcase to the breaking point, even with the expansion unzipped.

I was about to close it up when my eyes caught a glimpse of green draped over the chair in the corner. My eyes filled with tears.

I didn't know if Genevieve had meant to include the floral sundress from the Four Seasons Dance in her offer, but before I could think it over too much, I was digging out a black long-sleeve tee and tossing it aside to make room for the dress in my suitcase.

"Promise me you'll wear it with your boots," Genevieve said from the doorway.

I folded the dress in half. "Wouldn't think of wearing it any other way."

"Thought you might need some lemonade." She crossed to the dresser and set a glass on the top.

When she didn't move away, I looked up. I saw in her eyes a question I didn't want to answer. Maybe she sensed that because she didn't phrase it as a question.

"You could stay," she suggested.

Caught between laughing and bawling, I settled for shaking my head. "I couldn't."

"I wasn't wrong," she continued, "when I said you were good for each other."

I let out a slow breath. "And I wasn't wrong when I said he belonged here at the ranch."

"Maybe you do too," she said softly.

I wanted to argue. The Cassie who arrived here a month ago would have. She would have laughed at the very idea of staying in Texas, of feeling like she might ever actually belong on a working ranch.

But the Cassie who had just packed jeans and jerky into her carry-on was a less certain creature.

"I—" I began, but then realized this wasn't about me. Or, rather, it wasn't only about me. I was too tired and too emotionally taut to offer her anything but the truth. "He didn't ask me to stay."

"Of course not," she said, and I jerked back.

That was not the response I'd expected.

Her smile gentled. "Would you ask him to go?"

"No," I replied. "That wouldn't be fair, not when I know how much he loves the ranch."

"Then why would you think he would ask that sacrifice from you? He wouldn't want to force your hand, Cassie." Genevieve laid her hands on my shoulders, both reassuring and pleading. "In the same way I hated feeling like I made Ty move home, he wouldn't want to feel like he made you stay."

Her words made sense, but they didn't ease the sting.

I started to say something—to say I was scared, maybe, or uncertain. I might have even said yes.

But then reality smacked me upside the head. Why was I even considering this crazy idea? I had a career to—hopefully —get back to. I had plans and dreams and friends and a life. It was insanity to think about leaving all of that behind for... what? Ty and I hadn't made any promises to each other. We hadn't done more than enjoy each other's company for the space of a few weeks. I couldn't do a one-eighty on my life because I had a good time. Could I?

"It just..." I shook my head and took a step back. "It wouldn't work, Genevieve. This life isn't me."

From the look on her face, I think she knew I was trying to convince myself.

IF SOMEONE HAD TOLD ME, back when I first met Roughshod, that I would be sad to leave her when this was over, I would have handed them a ticket to crazytown. But as I walked up to her stall door—for the last time—I did so with an ache in my heart.

She lifted her head and stuck her muzzle through the bars.

"Do you think I have something for you?" I teased.

Her lips reached out, like some kind of velvety clam trying to catch a piece of passing plankton—or whatever clams ate.

"Okay, fine," I said, reaching into my pocket. "I do."

I held out the apple, careful to keep my palm flat as she greedily snatched it away. As she chomped loudly on the extra special treat, I reached through the bars and scratched her forehead.

I really was going miss her.

A weight settled against my thigh. I looked down at Babe, who leaned against me like I was a wall put there to hold her up. Or like she knew I was leaving.

She looked up at me, her soft brown eyes sad and droopy.

I sighed. "Yes, I suppose I'll miss you too."

She took that as an invitation and before I could blink, her paws were on my shoulders and I was struggling to stay upright.

"Babe!" Ty's voice snapped.

The big dog immediately dropped back to all fours and bounded down the aisle toward her master.

"She was fine," I said, forcing a smile. "I held my own this time."

He just looked at me for a moment and then said, "The car is loaded. Eddie is ready to go."

My smile faded as he turned and walked away. Babe stuck right on his heels, without even a glance back at me.

I made my way slowly down the aisle, and slower still up the dirt path to the house. With every step I felt the weight of my departure even more. No more earthy red dust. No more smell of cedar on the breeze. No more egg gathering or biscuit baking or baths in that amazing claw-foot tub.

Maybe I could beg Bethany to let me use hers every once in a while.

Everyone was gathered around the rented SUV. Eddie swung my suitcase into the back, on top of his—now—*two* duffle bags. He had my purse slung over his shoulder and the car keys clenched in his teeth.

"Fywawee," he said when he saw me. At my utterly confused expression, he spit the keys into his hand and repeated, "Finally. Let's go."

A flood of tears rushed to my eyes, but I blinked them away. Well, I blinked them back beneath the surface. I knew they weren't entirely gone. Just in hiding.

"Here," Genevieve said, pushing a small white box wrapped with a black ribbon covered in little white horse-shoes. "I made you some pralines for the road."

I took the box in one hand and grabbed her into a tight hug, carefully holding the pralines out of the way so I didn't bean her in the head.

"Thank you," I whispered in her ear. "For everything."

She squeezed me like she might never see me again. "You're always welcome to come back. Anytime."

I leaned away and gave her a watery smile. "You're always welcome on my couch," I replied. I held up the box. "And you can teach me how to make these when you move to New York."

She bit her lips, like she couldn't say any more.

"Thanks for the sweets, my sweet," Eddie called out as he climbed into the driver's seat.

Genevieve went around the car to say something to him, conveniently leaving me alone with Ty.

"You be careful out there, city gal." He jammed his hands in his back pockets.

I clutched the box of pralines. "I will." I nodded at the ranch lands behind him. "You be careful out there, cowboy."

In my mind, I imagined rushing forward and throwing my arms around his neck. Covering him with kisses while he spun me around in the afternoon sun.

In reality, I stared at the white box.

"Genevieve is right," Ty said carefully. "You're welcome anytime."

I held my breath, waiting for him to say more. To say he wanted me to come back, wanted me to stay. Wanted me to never leave again.

But he didn't.

So I replied, "Awesome. Great." And added, "Thanks for being so patient with me."

His hesitation made me look up. Though I couldn't read anything in his stormy blue eyes, the crinkles at the corners of his eyes made me smile.

"It was my pleasure," he finally said. "Thanks for bringing a spark of chaos to the Black Willow."

I couldn't help it. I rushed forward, wrapped my arms quickly around his neck, and whispered, "Anytime."

And then I was climbing into the car. Buckling my seatbelt. Placing the box of pralines carefully in my purse. Smoothing the legs of my jeans down over my boots.

Anything and everything not to have to watch the Black Willow disappear from view. Not to have to watch Ty disappear right along with it.

My tears came out of hiding in full force.

EIGHTEEN

THE LAST TIME I sat in Bud Gorman's office, he offered me the chance to redeem myself by producing the pilot episode of *Try It On*. The time before that, he'd been threatening to fire me for the disastrous end of *One Straight Guy at a Time*.

Honestly, I had no idea which time this visit would more resemble.

But as I sat on the uncomfortable chair facing his desk, my hands shook and I knew I was sweating through my layers of deodorant. I only hoped Bud couldn't tell from the safe distance across his desk.

"I don't give a rat's grass if she is Marilyn Monroe reincarnated," he barked into his phone, "she is not getting a private jet to fly her in from Queens."

He didn't wait for a response from the poor PA at the other end of the line.

I'd been in that position more times than I could count, caught between the talent and the power. It was not an enviable spot.

And yet, I'd rather have been there than here at the moment.

Bud ran a hand over his thinning hair. Judging from the scarlet tint of his skin, his blood pressure was higher than his doctors would like. Or maybe it had something to do with the contents of the coffee mug on the corner of his desk.

"I've seen the initial cut," he said, jarring me from my speculation about the state of his health.

I jumped, forcing myself to meet his stern gaze. Bud was fond of the stare-down technique, silently watching his victim until they blurted out something—anything—to break the tension. Usually something incriminating.

He would have made a formidable prosecutor.

Never show fear.

I hadn't seen the cut yet. I didn't even know if I would be allowed to. If I were fired on the spot, I would never get to see what Ty and I created together.

My heart thudded—not at the thought of getting fired, but at the thought of Ty.

I'd thought of him a million different times in the few days since I'd been back in New York. When I woke up with the sunrise, I wondered if he was already up and in the barn. When I pulled on my cowgirl boots, I thought of the Four Seasons dance. When I passed the Packing House and my way to meet Eddie for coffee yesterday… well I nearly broke down on the spot.

I dug my nails into my palms. I needed to get back in the moment.

"You had a lot of responsibilities to juggle on this shoot," Bud finally said.

"Yes sir."

He lifted one eyebrow. And when it didn't appear as though I was going to offer any additional thoughts, he said, "It looks good."

Every ounce of breath in my lungs heaved out in a massive sigh of relief.

"Really?" I said, then quickly corrected myself. "Good. Yes. Thank you."

After weeks of uncertainty, of stress and worry and not knowing whether it was all going to be enough in the end. After leaving Texas with no assurance that I was coming back to resume my career or start looking for a new one. I finally knew. It had all been worth it.

I couldn't wait to tell Ty.

Bud averted his gaze and started shuffling some papers around on his desk. He didn't look nervous so much as… considering.

"Consider yourself off probation, Bishop," he said. "The board greenlit the show. Filming on episode two starts a week from Monday. The production is yours, if you want it."

My breath caught in my throat. This was exactly what I'd been hoping for. Every time my jeans grew heavy with dust, every time rope rubbed my palms raw, every time I fell into bed literally exhausted from a long day of hard work, I had told myself it would be worth it in the end. It would be worth it, if it meant my career was back on track.

And now it was.

For several long moments I couldn't breathe. I couldn't speak. I couldn't even think.

Then, when I could, the first thought that sprang to mind was, *No*.

What? No, that wasn't right. I was supposed to be ecstatic.

I was supposed to be jumping up and down in my seat—on the inside—and saying, *Why yes, thank you,* in a very professional manner.

Instead, my stomach lurched and I had to bite my lips to keep from saying the answer I didn't want to give.

But I couldn't hold my tongue indefinitely. Bud was watching me, waiting for a reply.

I had to say yes. I had to accept, because there were dozens—hundreds—of other producers, aspiring and otherwise, lined up to take this gig if I turned it down. Which in no way explained why I wasn't leaping at the chance.

This was the big payoff I'd been waiting for. So why did it feel like a lead vice was tightening around my throat? Around my heart?

I tried to form an answer. "I am…"

Bud raised his thick, bushy brows. "I think the word you're looking for is some variation on *thrilled.*"

"Of course," I said. "I am. Thrilled, that is."

God, what was wrong with me? I'd been feeling off since I got back to New York, but this was beyond weird.

"Mr. Gorman," I began, completely planning on saying, *I would love the job,* but instead blurting, "Bud, can I have some time to think about it?"

No! That wasn't what I meant to say.

"I beg your pardon?"

"I just—" *Quick, Cassie. Scramble.* "This is a big decision, sir. And I want to make sure I'm considering it carefully."

He grumbled something unintelligible, shoved some more things around on his desk, and finally reached for the coffee mug in the corner and downed the contents in one swig. I jumped as he slammed the mug back down on the desk.

He jabbed a finger at the phone on his desk. "Marian, bring me more coffee."

"Right away, sir," a gentle voice said through the speaker.

"And add some whiskey!"

There was a pause and then, "Yes sir."

Bud then turned his attention back to me.

"You have until Monday, Bishop."

I nodded several times, as if reassuring myself that this would be okay. That I was just in shock after getting what I'd been stressing about for weeks. A kind of post-traumatic stress paralysis. That had to be it.

"Thank you, sir."

On my way out of the office, I passed Bud's long-suffering and borderline incompetent assistant. She gave me a weak smile and I tried to return it. But my mind was elsewhere. It was reeling, trying to figure out exactly what I hadn't grabbed the job the instant he offered it to me.

It was everything I'd been working for, everything I'd gone to Texas to achieve.

But the hollow ache in my gut wasn't content. And I'd never been very good at analyzing my gut.

"ARE YOU WEARING BLUSH?" Bethany asked as she took the seat across from me in the diner.

Her observant question only made my cheeks flame.

"And do you have a tan?"

"I don't tan," I answer. "And yes, I'm wearing blush."

Bethany's elegant brows lifted in surprise.

"Yes, okay," I blurt, "I'm wearing blush. The world is not ending."

She bit back a smile as she reached for the laminated menu.

Bethany was not usually a dive-y diner kind of girl, but I'd asked her to make an exception. I had less than twenty-four hours to give Bud my answer about the job and the only two things that could help me figure things out were Bethany and a thick, greasy patty melt.

After the waitress had taken our orders—without managing to look too shocked when my friend only ordered a salad with dressing on the side—Bethany leaned her elbows on the table, laced her fingers together, and leaned toward me.

"What's the matter, Cassie?" she asked. "You had your meeting with your boss on Friday, right? Did he not offer you the job?"

"That's the problem," I replied. "He *did*."

She scowled. "Then what exactly is the problem?"

"I didn't take it."

"You turned him down?"

"No," I said, jamming my fingers into my curls. "Not exactly. I asked for some time to make my decision. I have until tomorrow."

"And you haven't decided yet?"

I shook my head slowly.

The waitress arrived with my chocolate shake and Bethany's iced tea. While I took a long draw of frozen, creamy goodness, Bethany studied me over the rim of her glass.

"Tell me about Texas," she said in a curious tone.

"Texas?" I echoed. "Why? There's nothing to tell."

Bethany hummed into her tea.

"It was job," I offered. "I had a good time."

"And there was a guy?"

"Yes, but—" I shook my head. "It didn't work out. He's not interested in leaving Texas."

"Not a city guy then?"

I shrugged. "He actually used to live here. Went to City College and grad school. Then his parents died and he went home to help his sister run the family ranch."

Bethany swirled her straw in her tea, sending ice cubes clinking against the walls of the glass. I had always been more than a little jealous of her. She always looked so pulled together, always seemed so certain of what she wanted in life. And now, with her beloved Chris at her side, it looked like she was going to get it all on a platter.

Meanwhile I was struggling to muddle through.

I used to know what I wanted—at least I thought I did. A career in television. Reality television had never been exactly the ideal, but I loved the challenge and the ever-changing chaos of it. When I thought I was going to lost that career, I'd done everything I possibly good to get it back. And then I asked for more time.

"I just think…" I mused out loud. "I might be looking for something more."

"More than producing?"

"No." I sucked down a strawful of my shake. "More than reality TV. Do you remember when I used to make those mini-documentaries in college?"

Bethany laughed. "You were always filming something. Pizza night in the lounge. A squirrel digging up the south lawn." She set her glass down. "My favorite one was the sunrise supercut."

"Oh yeah. I'd forgotten that one."

Junior year, I had a room with an east facing window. I'd decided to film every single sunrise for the entire second semester. Then I'd edited them all together and sped up the frame rate so that four months of sunrises passed in just over ten minutes.

The result had been breathtaking.

That east facing window had been my inspiration. I'd felt the same creative pull at the Black Willow.

"I want to make more films like that," I explained. "Things that tap into my creative core."

I held a hand over my heart, like I could feel the sounds and images of future projects just waiting to find their way onto film.

"Your eye for the beautiful and the moving is undeniable." Bethany took another sip of her tea. "Are you thinking about leaving New York?"

She asked the question so casually I almost missed it, almost missed the implication. "What? No, of course not."

If there was one thing that defined me, it was that I was a New Yorker. Tried and true. Through and through. I've never wanted to live anywhere else.

"Clearly you found something in Texas that inspired you." She studied me with an unblinking gaze. "Or some*one*."

I opened my mouth to argue, but the words died in the back of my throat. She was right. Of course she was right. Whether it was the Texas outback or a certain Texas cowboy that inspired me, before I went to the Black Willow I'd been content to keep producing reality TV for the masses. By the time I left, I wanted more.

"Did you ask him to come back with you?" Bethany asked.

With a heavy sigh, I shook my head. "He loves the ranch. It wouldn't be fair to ask him to leave."

Bethany lifted her vibrant green eyes to spear me with a serious look. "Did he ask you to stay?"

Just like that, all my years of strength and refusal to cry except for extreme situations of loss or blood evaporated like dust above a gravel road. My eyes stung and my nose tingled.

"I'm sorry, honey," Bethany said.

Our waitress returned with our food. As Bethany dug into her rabbit food, I could only stare at my patty melt with disgust. Usually I dove onto the greasy, artery-clogger like a lifeboat in a flood, but today I looked at that thin brown-gray patty and all I could think about was the juicy one Genevieve had cooked up on one of my last nights in Texas. How could the beef here in the city ever compare with ranch-fresh fare I'd gotten used to at the Black Willow?

Was I doomed to spend the rest of my life comparing New York to my time in Texas?

I grabbed my knife and fork and began cutting the sandwich into smaller bites, in case that might make it more appetizing.

"Not hungry?" Bethany asked between forkfuls of salad.

I shrugged. "I had a really great patty melt recently." I pushed a soggy square around on my plate. "I don't think this one can compare."

This sandwich was almost slimy, not like Genevieve's perfectly juicy version.

The memory of the trickle of that juice glistening at the corner of Ty's mouth filled my mind, of how I'd instinctively reached to wipe it away and how he'd captured my wrist and pulled me in for a kiss in front of the whole table. In that moment, with his mouth on mine, everything had felt right.

Bethany and I ate in silence for several minutes. I was too distracted by my own thoughts to realize how odd it was for her to go so long without speaking. But when she finally finished with her salad and pushed the bowl away, she started with a doozy.

"Do you love him?"

I didn't look up from my plate. "Yes."

"Would you move there for him?"

I nodded.

"Then why don't you?"

Finally I met her gaze. "He didn't ask me to stay. What if he doesn't want me to."

"What if he just didn't want to hear you say no."

"What's the difference?"

"Maybe a big one."

I shook my head. "If he loved me, he would have at least asked."

"You didn't ask him to leave."

"It's not the same," I insisted.

"Isn't it?"

Another shake.

"Did you tell him how you feel?"

"No," I admitted.

"You're scared," Bethany guessed. "You're afraid that he doesn't feel the same way. That you'll take a big risk and it'll slap you in the face."

I titled my head back and stared at the asbestos tile ceiling. Bethany's hand closed over mine and squeezed.

"The thing is," she said softly, "everything in life is a risk. It's just a matter of whether you think it's worth it. Is it?"

Part of me wanted to scream yes, to insist that Ty was worth any potential heartbreak. But the fear held me back.

"That's the decision you'll have to make. You have to risk your heart to win his."

I gave her a small, sad smile. What if I was too scared to try?

NINETEEN

MY HEART REMAINED SURPRISINGLY steady as I walked into Bud's office. The last three times I had been in here were pure stress. First, getting dressed down for the disaster on *One Straight Guy*. Second, getting my probationary assignment to produce the pilot episode of *Try It On*. And finally, the last time, when he had praised my work and offered me my dream job. I hadn't known going in whether it would be good or bad, and so I'd been more than a little freaking out.

This time, though, I felt completely under control. For the first time in a long time—maybe since the day I decided to become a film major and forge my career in this crazy industry —I was in charge of my own future. I was responsible for my own destiny.

The job was mine to take. Or leave.

Everything was in my hands.

Maybe I should have been freaking out more. My entire future might rest on the decision I made when I walked through those doors. But for some reason… I felt at peace.

And the craziest part was that I still wasn't entirely, one-hundred-percent certain what I was going to say. I knew what I wanted to say, what I thought I should say. I just didn't know if that was what would come out of my mouth at the given time.

Bud held up a finger as I walked in. "You tell him," he barked into the phone, "that he either shows up bright eyed and bushy-friggin-tailed tomorrow or I will sue him for breach of contract faster than he can say action."

I smiled. As I sank into the chair across from Bud's desk, I felt my entire body relax. In that instant, I knew my answer. I believed in it.

Bud slammed the receiver down and jabbed the intercom button. "Bring me a scotch, Marian. Two fingers. Neat." He leaned back in his chair and ran a hand through nonexistent hair. "Jesus, these foreign directors drive me up a friggin wall."

I waited patiently as Bud's assistant brought in a glass of scotch for her boss and a bottle of water for me. I flashed her a grateful smile as she swept back out of the room.

The scotch was gone by the time I turned back to face the desk.

"Better," Bud gasped, slamming the glass back down on the desk. "Now, let's talk details. Filming has been pushed back. You've got six weeks. You'll need to be on location in Bermuda in four, with casting for episode two finalized by next Friday. We've already got the crew signed on, but if you have any requests—"

"I'm not taking the job."

Bud jerked back, his face twisting into a look of total confusion. He quickly recovered.

"You're right." He leaned forward to brace his elbows on the desk. "This show is a dog. One and done. You're better off on *Wall Street Wives*. That's got tabloid scandals written all over it. Five seasons, at least."

"No, Bud," I said with a deep sigh. "I mean, I'm not taking *any* job."

"You're sick of reality shows," he said. "I get it. How about a sitcom? We just started development on one about math geeks at MIT."

"No—"

"Drama?" Bud tried. "My nephew's got a pilot script for a new legal series."

"Bud, stop."

It was flattering, for sure, to be offered my choice of projects. After being on increasingly rocky ground over the past few months, it was nice to know that I had my pick of shows at Go Gorman Studios. That my career was back on the upward trajectory.

Too bad it was headed for a destination I didn't want to reach anymore.

"I—" I shook my head, trying to figure out how to explain this. In the end, simpler was better. "I'm going back to Texas."

He scowled at me. "Is this about the cowboy?"

"Yes," I said. "And no. It's about me. It's about the pace of life I want to lead and the kind of art I want to create."

Bud laughed. "Spoiled housewives and nerd humor aren't cutting it?"

"Not even a little."

He reached over and punched the intercom again. "Two drinks."

This time when Marian came in, she set a second glass of scotch in front of me.

"When you first applied for this job—" Bud raised his

glass, and I did the same. "—I knew you weren't a lifer. You had stars in your eyes."

"Stars?" I asked.

Bud threw back his scotch. "Okay, not stars. Oscars, maybe. Or the Spirit Awards. Cannes and Sundance at the very least."

I had been right out of film school, eager to get my foot in the door. I'd thought the production gig would be an on-ramp. It had turned into a parking spot. I loved the work. I loved being in charge of the production, making sure everything ran smoothly, and being the go-to-girl for every crisis in the making.

The problem was that I didn't believe in the product. Not anymore. Maybe I never had.

"I don't know about that," I said, "but I do know that I need to do something more meaningful." I pressed my still-full glass against my heart. "Something that fills me in here."

Bud nodded. He stared into his now-empty glass for several long seconds. It wasn't like him to be quiet. "If you ever need a backer," he finally said with uncharacteristic gentleness, "you have my number."

Now it was my turn to jerk back. Gone was the gruff, demanding, at times almost demeaning boss who had ridden my butt since the day I started working for him. Instead, I was looking at a man who genuinely believed in me and who, despite the fact that I was walking away from the job, wanted the best for me.

Surprise didn't come close to covering it.

"I appreciate the offer." I smiled as my eyes tingled. "And I appreciate every opportunity you've ever given me. You gave me wings, and now it's my time to fly."

"Wings?" He huffed, like he was disgusted by the sentiment, but his eyes got a little glassy before he looked away. "Now finish that drink before I take it all back."

I downed it in one gulp.

I'd just walked away from an open ticket to any job in television I could possibly want. It might take more than one drink to keep me going.

❤

ADRENALINE STILL PUMPED through my bloodstream when I got back to my apartment. Not only because I had turned down the job—but also that. Definitely that.

No, I was freaking out more than a little because of the decisions I'd made on my subway ride home.

I'd been standing there, squeezed into the corner between the door between cars and the conductor's cabin, the crush of rush hour commuters making the un-air-conditioned car beyond miserable, and I had an epiphany. I wanted fresh air.

And not just because the man who was pressed up against my back smelled like he'd been rolling around in a dirty horse stall. I wanted to be able to walk out my front door and breathe in the smells of earth and nature instead of exhaust and garbage. I wanted to be able to roll down the window on my way from here to there, not be trapped inside an airless subway car with a thousand other people.

In short, I wanted Texas.

I wanted Texas, and I wanted to film every minute of it.

That, I realized, was what didn't sit right with me about *Try It On*. The transition was only temporary. After the four weeks were over, the trier went back to the same old life. It wasn't a real experience. It wasn't real change.

I wanted that real change.

There was a precedent for my plans. Women across the country gobbled up Pioneer Woman's documentation of her journey from city girl to country life. What she did in a blog and a cooking show, I wanted to do documentary style. Maybe it would never see the light of day, but for me it was going to be about the journey. The end result didn't matter so much.

I'd spent the rest of my ride and the walk from the station to my building making lists. Equipment I need to acquire. Arrangements I needed to make. People I needed to inform. I had a lot of phone calls to make.

But my first one needed to be to Ty.

Avoiding the deathtrap elevator in my building, I raced up the stairs to my apartment, eager to get started on my new plan. As I crested the landing on my floor, I pulled out my keys and my phone.

"You're wearing your boots."

I screamed and dropped my keys. Which, if it had been a legitimate mugging, would have been the worst thing I could do since my safety whistle and mini can of mace were attached to my keyring.

Ty stepped out of the shadows across the hall from my apartment door.

"I didn't mean to scare you," he said.

Hand pressed to my exploding chest, I replied breathlessly, "You didn't."

He laughed and I wanted to fling myself across the hall and into his arms. We stared at each other, and I wondered if my eyes looked as hungry to take him in as his did looking at me. Had it only been a week since I left him in Texas? It felt like a lifetime.

I visually devoured him—from his cowboy boots to his Yankees cap.

"I was going to call you," I said.

His mouth kicked up to one side. "That sounds like a line."

"No really." I couldn't keep the silly smile off my face. "Right now. I was about to walk inside and call you."

I held up my phone in evidence.

"Really?" his voice dropped to an innuendo-laden tone. "What were you going to say?"

My already-racing heart rate doubled. I thought I would have a little more time to prepare myself to say the words. I thought I'd be saying them over the phone, not face-to-face. I wasn't sure if this made it easier or harder.

To buy myself some time, I motioned to the door. I didn't want this conversation on front-and-center display for my already nosy neighbors. When we were inside, standing in my kitchen, I finally answered.

"They greenlit the show."

Ty's expression fell. That wasn't what I'd intended to say, but I was getting used to the breakdown in communication between my brain and my tongue.

He smiled half-heartedly. "That's great. So you got the job?"

I drew in a fortifying breath. "I got the offer."

His blue eyes sparked. He hadn't missed my implication.

"I turned it down."

The smile returned, broadened, and dimples appeared in his cheeks. "Did you?"

I nodded.

"And why is that?" He stepped closer.

The moment of truth. Literally.

"Because I love Texas."

His dimples deepened and he moved closer still, until only inches separated us. "Anything else?"

I nodded again.

"Let me guess." He lifted his hand to trace his fingertips over my cheek. "You missed Roughshod."

"And Babe," I said as I laid my hands on his chest. "And Genevieve's chickens."

"And that coyote outside your window?" His head dipped lower.

"Definitely the coyote."

I lifted onto my toes and pressed my mouth to his. As his heat spread into me, as our breath met and mingled, as that gentle pressure sealed us together, my anxiety faded into oblivion. When he pulled back enough put a millimeter of space between us, I sighed the happiest sigh.

"I love you, Ty Haywood," I whispered.

I felt his smile against my lips. "I love you, too, Cassie Bishop."

"Even though I'm a city gal?"

His arms slipped around my waist and pulled me closer. "Because you're a city gal."

"So if I wasn't one," I teased, "you wouldn't love me anymore?"

"That depends. What would you be instead?"

"A cowgirl," I replied. "Definitely a cowgirl."

"In that case…" His arms tightened around me. "I might love you even more."

I kissed him again. And then, suddenly, it was twenty minutes later.

Before we got carried away—correction, before we got even

more carried away, I wanted to tell him about my plans. I gave him a rundown of my plan to sublet my apartment, to film my transition, to give myself a fresh start in the country.

"It should only take me a few days to get everything squared away," I explained. "I don't have that much to pack. With you here to help, it will go even faster."

His eyebrows frowned together. "I can't stay," he said. "We have a group of visitors arriving tomorrow afternoon, so I'm on the redeye back tonight."

"Oh." My mood fell a few notches, but I reminded myself I would only be here a few days. We wouldn't be separated for long. "That's okay. I'll take care of all the details and then I'll join you on the Black Willow."

His smile had that mischievous look that I usually only saw in his sister.

"Actually…" he said, his voice a mix of smile and smirk, "there's a second ticket on the redeye in your name."

My jaw dropped. "You were that confident I would be coming back with you?"

"Hopeful," he said, shaking his head. "Hopeful, city gal. It would only be a couple days, until I'm sure everything is set up for the visitors. I know it's short notice—"

"I have to pack!" My heart jumped at the chance to get back to the ranch that much sooner. Packing and sublets and utilities and mail forwarding could come later. I dashed for my bedroom. "This might take a while."

"You've only been back a week," he said with a laugh as he followed on my heels. "How bad could it—"

He froze mid-sentence when I opened the door.

My bedroom could not have looked more disastrous if a hurricane swirled up the stairs, blew into my apartment, and took up residence here for several weeks. It had been a wreck when I left for Texas and had only gotten worse since my return.

"That's impressive."

I shoved against his chest, pushing him back into the hall. "Just go have a seat in the living. I'll be out as soon as I can."

"I'll be..." He backed slowly away from the door. "Just holler if you need any help."

I smiled as he retreated. No, I didn't need any help. I just needed ten minutes and a ticket to Texas.

TWENTY

THE FIRST TIME I left New York for Texas, my stomach was full of dread. And nausea. And a city-sized ball of stress. I'd been being torn away from my beloved city, from the life I had carefully built from drive and ambition. This time was different.

I reached over and took Ty's hand as the plane started down the runway.

He smiled. "Are you—"

"Don't ask me if I'm sure," I interrupted before he could finish his question. "I am."

One side of his mouth kicked up to the side.

"What?" I asked.

The plane roared down the runway. Ty shook his head and leaned back into his seat. I leaned across him to look out the window, to say goodbye to my city.

Not forever, I knew. New York would only be a plane ride away—or two or seven, depending on the weather in the Midwest. But I was equal parts excited and terrified. It wasn't about leaving the city, it was about leaving the life I thought I wanted. The life I'd spent so many years working toward. The life that had been gnawing at me from the inside out, making me rush through every day like I was headed for some invisible finish line.

The life that one stint on a ranch in Texas taught me wasn't the life I wanted after all.

I sighed and leaned back in my seat. The idea of leaving behind the slightly-less-risky world of reality show production for the risky-beyond-belief world of independent film and documentary production was… No, not terrifying. Exhilarating.

No, definitely terrifying, too. I was going to regret not bringing any antacids.

I smiled and squeezed Ty's hand. "What were you going to ask me?"

"Are you *sure*," he began, and I smacked him on the shoulder. He turned a cocky smirk on me. "Are you sure you don't want the window?"

Tilting my head against his shoulder, I didn't bother answering. I didn't need to see what I was leaving behind, and I already knew where I was going. For once, I took a deep breath and enjoyed being exactly where I was in that moment.

Dear reader,

Originally, the third City Chicks book was going to be Fiona's story. But after writing about Cassie in *Straight Stalk*, I just knew her story had to be next. And so, *Trying Texas* was born.

After writing several young adult books, I had a blast going back into the chick lit world of this series. I hope you enjoyed reading it as much as I loved writing it! Even if you didn't, please take a moment to leave a **review**. It means a lot!

The City Chicks series began with candy-obsessed fashion executive Lydia's story in *Eye Candy*. Turn the page for a sneak peek…

To get insider extras, exclusive giveaways, and breaking news, visit teralynnchilds.com/subscribe to join my mailing list.

Tera L. Childs

EYE CANDY
Chapter 1

My lower left desk drawer holds a secret.

Looking at the rest of my office you'd never guess. The pristine mahogany surface of the desk is unspoiled by dust or clutter. Every office tool has a place and every file is appropriately color coded. Rows of sales data binders are neatly aligned and in chronological order. The flat-panel monitor is oriented at the perfect ergonomic angle to minimize eye strain and glare.

But that drawer—securely locked if I'm out of the office for even a second—is the exception to my immaculately professional appearance.

That drawer is loaded with candy.

A sweet-tooth soup of peppermints, lemon drops, butterscotches, caramels, lollipops, and atomic fireballs. A treasure trove of red vines, gummy bears, licorice whips, fruit slices, red hots, and tropical dots stacked in disorderly piles.

My name is Lydia Vanderwalk, and I'm a candy-holic.

I've known this for a long time and freely confess my dependency. I know I couldn't stop, even if I wanted to.

I would never, ever want to.

I live for the sugar rush of a one-pound bag of M&Ms. Sour apple tape got me through my college all-nighters. Every great idea I ever had was Lifesavers-induced.

When I was four years old, my mom dressed me as Jo from *Facts of Life* and took me trick-or-treating. Everyone thought I was Michael J. Fox. I was traumatized. When we got home I dumped my booty onto the carpet and started consuming. Amongst the Smarties and fun-size Snickers I found comfort for my costume identity crisis. Candy soothed my pain. And has ever since.

Next Halloween I was a gumdrop. Not one nearsighted neighbor mistook me for a pink mountain.

Candy is my coping mechanism, and it's less destructive than other addictions I could have. As far as vices go, it's a harmless one.

In my industry, though, it's the eighth mortal sin. People in fashion—correction, *women* in fashion don't eat anything, let alone candy by the bucketful. That's why my secret could never get out.

Thankfully, I am skilled at maintaining the appearance of normalcy.

So when Janice, junior VP of Marketing for Ferrero Couture and my direct superior (otherwise mentally known as Jawbreaker—hard on the outside hard on the inside) barged into my office without so much as a knock on the closed door, I slipped open the drawer, pulled out a Werther's, and popped it in my mouth.

She was dressed, as usual, like an aging Vegas cigarette

girl. Shoulder-padded silver blazer with a deep-v neckline, tight black pants, and eye makeup that made Cleopatra look like a bare-faced virgin. She thinks she's the Donatella Versace of Ferrero Couture. She's an executive, for Good&Plenty's sake —a design diva she is not.

In my grey, summer wool pantsuit and lilac cashmere shell I felt deliciously like Belgian chocolate next to a bag of carob chips.

"Have you seen the new *GQ*?" she asked.

"*Uh-uh*," I hummed around the toffee. The buttery sweetness melted into my tongue and improved my overall sense of well-being.

She plunked the magazine on my desk and smirked. I flicked my eyes to the cover and back to her, trying to maintain an air of nonchalance and disguise my annoyance at her intrusion. My gaze flew immediately back to the slick image on the glossy cover. *Gavin*!

Now Jawbreaker's smirk made sense.

Here came conversation #3,524—not that I'm counting— about the Lamentable Loss of Gavin the Great.

"Isn't this your fiancé, Lydia?" she said, gloating. "Oops, I mean your *ex*-fiancé."

Right, that was a slip-up.

If I could manage to scalp her hip-length platinum tresses and braid them into a fashionable tiara without getting fired, I would. That might even become the next hot trend from Ferrero Couture. But as that was a remote possibility, I held my tongue and started mentally ranking my favorite Jelly Belly flavors.

Toasted Marshmallow, Cotton Candy, Buttered Popcorn...

I smiled politely.

…Green Apple, Juicy Pear, Strawberry Cheesecake…

"Imagine all the women chasing after him now."

My smile fake-brightened.

…Crushed Pineapple, Watermelon, Grape Jelly…

"Have you tried to get in touch with him? Maybe there's still a chance—"

I had to stop her before my head exploded and a rainbow of Skittles drizzled down over my immaculate office. "Haven't I told you,"—Jawbreaker—"Janice, about the new guy I've been seeing?"

I regretted those words almost before they left my mouth. Lying was not my strength, but when Jawbreaker started down the Gavin path, I couldn't help myself. So I came up with the one thing sure to stop her in her tracks: a boyfriend.

Unfortunately, she was a seasoned social veteran and her path changed faster than you can say Reese's Pieces.

"How wonderful," she cried, not meaning it at all. "You simply must bring him to the Summer Sail Away next weekend."

Summer Sail Away, my mind echoed. The end of summer gala at Jawbreaker's Southampton *tres* posh estate—her husband owns a ridiculously successful import/export busi-ness. *The* fashion industry event of the season. All the senior VPs will be there. All the board members will be there. Ferrero will be there. Half the fashion world will be there.

Never before had I been graced with an invitation.

As senior account exec, my social profile never ranked high enough to warrant an invite. And, since my status had not recently changed, I had to assume Jawbreaker thought she was pulling one over on me.

Show up stag after the whole extremely small world of

fashion heard about this new beau? It would be poor, pitiful Lydia. And a liar to boot.

I could always not show up.

But I wanted a promotion. A rumor had been circling that Jawbreaker was about to be promoted to senior VP of Marketing. And I would do anything to get her current job. The gala would give me the chance to prove I was more than a brain with a knack for numbers. A chance to show Ferrero that I was VP material and could schmooze with the best of them.

A chance I couldn't pass up.

With the KY Clique—my trio of nemeses at Ferrero—out to get my current job I had to seize opportunities where I could.

"Wonderful," I replied, knowing my farce was worth it just to see the scowl crease Jawbreaker's brow. Botox can't fix everything. "What time should we be there?"

♥

Kelly showed up first. She was the most aggressive of the three KY girls—the team leader—and Jawbreaker probably ran to her with the gossip of my previously unheard of boyfriend the moment she left my office.

The KY Clique came on board at Ferrero as marketing interns in May following their Barnyard—er, Barnard graduation. From the start they settled for nothing less than full control of the house. I have an under-the-table wager with Marlene in accessories that the house will be Ferrero, Kelly, Kathryn & Karyn within five years. Three if they stumbled onto a stroke of luck or juicy gossip.

And I might have just handed them that lucky gossip on a jewel-encrusted silver platter.

Kelly knocked—the simple courtesy the first sign she was up to something—and entered on the pretense of needing my opinion on an overseas marketing campaign. A blatant ruse as my region covers the western United States.

"Oh," she squealed as I tried to not-so-subtly urge her out of my office. "Janice told me about your new boyfriend. He sounds like a prince."

That's funny, because I don't remember telling Jawbreaker anything about him. Because I don't know anything about him. Because he doesn't exist.

"I mean, it's not as if just *anyone* can measure up to Gavin, but a girl's gotta try, right?"

"Mmm-hmm." Hopefully a vague enough response to derail conversation #3,525—not that I'm counting.

I'm never that lucky.

"It's about time you moved on to someone new. Two years is far too long for someone your age to stay single. You need to do your hunting before all the big game are shot."

Like I need relationship advice from a preschooler.

Her monologue didn't warrant any input on my part, so I contented myself with neatening up a stack of papers on my desk while she talked on.

"I can't believe you never mentioned this new guy before. He must be something special if you've been keeping him all to yourself," she cooed. "And we all get to meet him at the Summer Sail Away."

Suppressing the sudden and overwhelming urge to scream, I lunged for my candy drawer. Within seconds I had a Melt-away in my mouth. The sweet sugary goodness could almost make up for the news that the KYs—low chicks in the hen house—were already invited to the Summer Sail Away. It took me a fabricated boyfriend and an ex on the cover of *GQ* to earn one.

Clearly I should have gone to Barnard. Maybe if I changed my name to Kydia…

"Hi Kelly," twin high-pitched voices squealed.

Kathryn and Karyn bounded into my office. I was surrounded by KYs with no means of escape.

They looked so similar. They could be triplets, with their matching golden highlights, colorful wrap dresses, and stiletto slingbacks. I could usually tell them apart by their nails—Kathryn was natural and unpolished, Karyn was French-manicured, while Kelly was all-acrylic and more than a little scary around ripe fruit.

"We heard about the new boyfriend,"—I checked the nails—Karyn exclaimed.

"Shame on you for keeping him a secret,"—unpolished—Kathryn chastised.

"But," Kelly interrupted, "he'll be at the Summer Sail Away."

"Ooh, I can't wait."

"We can evaluate his TIP for you."

His what? I needed a KY-to-English dictionary.

"His Total Income Potential. Maybe his TIP will be almost as high as Gavin's."

"Not likely!"

I gave up trying to figure out which one spoke. Dizzy, I desperately grabbed for another Meltaway.

I felt like a spectator at my own execution. Only I had handed the man in the black hood the axe and pulled my hair out of the way as I laid my head on the block.

Mental Post-It: Stop making up non-existent boyfriends.

"That's your ex?"

I looked up from the engrossing occupation of swirling ice in my Lemon Drop to find Fiona clutching *GQ* to her chest. One grape-lacquered finger stabbing at the cover.

Next to Fiona I always felt like the worst sort of invisible person. No style. No flare. No taste.

Tonight she wore a dark-washed denim pencil skirt over Limeade green fishnets with a silver sequined tank and metallic silver gladiator sandals. With her exotic looks and flare for fashion, everyone noticed when she enters a room.

"Nice to see you, too," I replied, thinking it's not really so nice if the conversation was heading where I thought it was heading.

Not in the mood to launch into conversation #3,527—not that I'm counting—I downed the remains of my drink and signaled Bartender Barbie to bring another. Conversation #3,524 had gotten me into enough trouble today and I didn't need any more bad JuJu.

"No, really," Fiona exclaimed, dropping her corduroy satchel next to the bar stool and lifting herself up onto the seat. *"This* is the man who broke your heart?"

I turned my best Westchester glare on her, but Fiona is a force of nature and proceeded without pause.

"He's gorgeous, babe. And rich. And successful. And—"

Gee, all things I didn't already know about him, having been engaged to the man for nearly six years. "Thanks, Fi. That makes me feel much better."

Bartender Barbie set another Lemon Drop in front of me

and gave me a look resembling pity. Great, my life was complete.

"The article gushes on about how he's this hotshot investment banker at Castile and Tatum, the youngest ever to make upper management."

Didn't Fiona notice my head banging desperately against the polished wood surface of the bar? Too engrossed in the details of my former—though I prefer to call him my late—fiancé, she didn't even care that I lost several strands of light brown hair to the sticky surface.

And, typical of the way my day had gone, I was not even lucky enough to knock myself unconscious.

"Why is Lydia already passed out?" a lilting Southern voice asked.

Bethany! Thank you Mr. Goodbar, I was saved.

Fiona peered over the magazine, surprised to see my face stuck to the bar. "Don't know," she mused, returning her attention to *GQ*.

Some girlfriend.

"I'm stuck," I managed to say, sounding even more pathetic than I felt, if possible.

"Let me help you, honey." Beth set her purse carefully on a stool before grabbing me by the shoulders and yanking.

That girl is stronger than she looks.

"Thanks." Cheek burning, I was now the only woman in the history of skin care to be exfoliated by a sticky bar counter. But at least I was upright.

Beth smiled before climbing gingerly onto the stool and smoothing out the wrinkles in her floral sundress. "What's the matter, sugar?"

Bartender Barbie brought her a Mojito before she had a

chance to order. I tried to forget that Barbie never remembered my drink order, even after two years of Friday nights.

Bethany looked like the typical southern belle. Tasteful but flirty floral sundress, sweet high heel Mary Janes, hose. Her long blonde hair meticulously curled and sprayed yet touchably soft. Guys jumped to be chivalrous for her. Everywhere she went doors opened before her, chairs got pulled out beneath her, and men fell to their knees begging for marriage.

But she did have that steel magnolia edge. She owned and operated a very successful shop in SoHo, and a sweet gal didn't last long in the city without learning to bite back.

"Oh my heavens," Beth exclaimed as she got a good look at the magazine in Fiona's clutches, "that's Gavin!"

"Yeah," Fiona answered, dropping the magazine to her lap. "Hot, huh?"

Beth will defend me. We've been friends since freshman year at Columbia, since before Gavin and I started dating. She knew his true nature—the sour, sticky core at his center.

I was wrong.

Beth nodded, taking a sip of her mojito. "Grade A Prime."

"I wouldn't mind rolling over to that the morning after." Fiona got a dreamy look, glitter-glossed lips grinning, that reminded me how much steamier her love life was than mine.

The conversation turned dangerous. In my experience, no woman is safe even fantasizing about Gavin Fairchild. I had to interject before someone got hurt. "Too bad he's such a Sour Apple Blow Pop."

Fiona was undeterred. "Does he have an agent?"

"An agent? Fi, he's a stockbroker."

"Yes, but he's a stockbroker on the cover of *GQ*."

I really shouldn't have been surprised. Fiona was a talent

agent at Famous Faces, after all. Representing the most delicious hunks on the planet was her daily duty. Which was great, so long as this was one delicious hunk she stayed far, far away from. For all our sakes.

Just as I opened my mouth to say as much, a realization struck: What did I care if Fiona represented Gavin to supermodel stardom? I didn't care about him. He was nothing but an anomaly in my otherwise normal dating record. He was the past. Good riddance to stale candy.

What I did care about was how everyone still treated me like I'd lost the winning lottery ticket. Gavin Fairchild was not my one and only chance at happily ever after.

Too bad I didn't realize this sooner. Like this afternoon. Like before Jawbreaker brought him up in conversation and I freaked. I freaked and now I was in such a tight fix that conversation #3,527—not that I'm counting—seemed like a shopping spree at Dylan's Candy Bar.

My groan, followed by the loud thunk as my head hit the bar again, must have caught Fiona and Beth's attention because each grabbed a shoulder and hauled me back up.

"What's wrong, sugar?"

"Tell us," Fiona urged.

"We can help," Beth promised.

"No," I said, recalling every appalling word of the conversations #3,524—not that I'm counting—and #3,525—not that I'm—oh, who was I kidding, I'm counting, "you can't."

Beth smiled. "Try us."

Resigned to the fate of relating every horrifying detail, I began my tale. As the words came out they picked up speed, and soon I was babbling about Jawbreakers, KYs, Southampton, and my desire to be a barnyard animal.

Fiona and Beth smiled and nodded and I could tell they wondered what in Hershey's name I was talking about.

The vodka in my Lemon Drops—plural—must have been getting to me. But confection was good for the soul and I couldn't stop.

"I had to shut her up," I continued between gulps of lemon-flavored alcohol. "I mean there's only so much ex-hashing a girl can take." Closing my eyes I pictured Jawbreaker, hip-length platinum hair twisting around one finger as she fantasized about Gavin right before my eyes. "So I told her I had a new guy."

Without looking, I felt them both shrug.

"I told her I had been dating this guy for several months and we're really getting serious. Seemed like a good idea at the time. Shows Gavin is forgotten and I'm moving on with my life, love and all. Until the unthinkable happened. Jawbreaker insists I bring him to the Summer Sail Away next weekend."

"Summer Sail Away?" Fiona's brow crinkled.

"*The* company function of the season at her mansion in Southampton." I groaned at the thought of losing my coveted promotion to a KY. "If I show up without this dream guy, my career is history."

"Why?" Beth inquired. "It's just a date."

"Jawbreaker would relish any excuse to humiliate me." And promote one of the KY Clique in my place. The bonds of Barnyard sisterhood are hard to break.

"We can find you a guy, no problem," Fiona announced.

"Oh yes," Beth added. I heard the excitement in her voice as my datelessness became her new project. "There's a guy in my building, Harvard grad, gorgeous to boot. He's perfect for you."

"No," I interjected adamantly. "I don't want a smart, gorgeous, lovable guy. No one interested in a relationship."

I was one busy Marshmallow Peep. My life was too full and too complicated already, without the added attachment of a guy.

Unfortunately, everyone in my life interpreted this independent streak as evidence of my pining for Gavin.

Beth smiled sadly. "It's been two years, sugar. Time to move on."

"I know. And I am," I insisted. "I have. But not right now. I have too much going on at work to get emotionally involved with anyone. I don't *need* a relationship."

Somehow, I couldn't bring myself to say that I didn't *want* a relationship. Rotten emotional longing. Stay under cover where you belong.

A look passed between my friends that I chose to interpret as concern, and I also chose to ignore it.

"Forget it. I'll just show up stag and weather Jawbreaker's interrogation."

"No, no, let us help." Resolve hardened Fiona's exotic features and I knew argument was futile.

I turned to Bethany, the face of a true steel magnolia.

"We'll find you the perfect guy," Beth promised.

"A trophy date."

"A date without a relationship."

"A man without opinions."

"Without emotions."

"Without baggage."

"Without a brain."

Coming to the bottom of my—third—Lemon Drop, I began to see possibilities. A guy for show. One that looks good and thinks little. Easy on the eyes and short on the intellect.

I grinned. "Eye candy."

We three stared at our drinks, deep in thought. Fiona finally spoke. "I know a guy."

"You know a guy?" I asked.

"From the agency, one of the models." Fiona paused. "He's looking for some extra cash, and..."

"And...?" I prodded.

"He's gorgeous and sweet. A little light in the attic but heavy in the basement, if you know what I mean." Fiona waggled her eyebrows.

I had no idea what she meant. But that might have been due to the Lemon Drops, so I gave her a shrug-nod and signaled for another drink.

"I'm sure he'd be willing to help you out," she continued. "For adequate compensation."

Whoa! Compensation? Have I reached the lowest of the low? Do I have to buy a date? And Fiona was selling me one. "You're pimping your models."

She shook her head, taking a sip of her Slow Comfortable Screw Up Against A Wall before continuing. "Just one model. Singular. And I'm not pimping, just arranging. Like a dating service where money changes hands."

"Sounds like pimping to me," I grumbled.

"Sounds like the perfect plan," Beth countered.

Had I thought earlier my day couldn't get any worse? Mental Post-It: Always anticipate something even more horrific happening.

"Sugar, this is everything you need," she persisted. "One gorgeous, boss-impressing hottie to get everyone off your back about Gavin and yourself out of the hole you've dug. One stringless guy who will accept your money at the end of the day and leave your heart intact."

Barbie set the fresh Lemon Drop before me, but I decided I had enough. This plan was starting to sound like a good idea—that had to be an alcohol-induced opinion.

"Look, give him a shot." Fiona dragged her satchel off the floor and pulled out her hot pink phone. A few taps of the screen and she announced, "He's doing an in-house shoot tomorrow. I'll talk to him and make all the arrangements. If he doesn't take, you can always publicly break up with him at the Sailboat Saga."

"Summer Sail Away," I corrected.

"Everyone will think you're hot stuff if you're too good for the likes of him." She shoved her phone back in her satchel.

"I don't think..."

"You're desperate. Take a chance."

Tired and fed up with feeling like a spectator in my own life, I took a stand.

"No."

Fiona and Beth peered at each other, brows raised. Maybe it was the vodka talking. Maybe it was the culmination of my horrendous day. Maybe it was me finally deciding to have a say in my own life. Whatever the case, they looked surprised.

But remained determined.

"You'll change your mind," Fiona stated.

With a groan, my forehead plunked to the bar.

Reehn, reehn, reehn!

"Uungh." I rolled over and slapped the alarm clock into silence. How dare it wake me up at 8:00 on a Saturday morning? Nine minutes later it started screaming again. Another slap. Another nine minutes later it started screaming again. This time, I pried open one desert dry eye and managed to find the off switch.

Ring, ring, ring.

"Nooo," I moaned.

There was no way I was prepared to speak. I let voicemail pick up.

My head felt like someone stuffed it full of gumballs—every movement sent the throbbing pain thundering to another side of my brain. My eyelids were stuck to my eyeballs, something that should have been medically impossible. And my stomach—well, let's just say my stomach was seriously rethinking everything I had consumed in the last twelve hours.

Having no desire to see any of that again, I sank into the softness of my feather-top and held a white downy pillow over my face.

Ring, ring, ring.

Even through the sound-baffling pillow I heard the phone.

I ignored it, ready to drift peacefully back to sleep. But as I started to doze my phone dinged. A message. Without opening my eyes, I played it.

There were actually two.

First message, Friday, 7:07 p.m.: "Hi, Lydia." Holy Hot Tamales. I jolted upright in bed. "It's Gavin. We need to talk. I know this is out of the blue, but can we get together this week? Call me, I can make time whenever you're available."

I replayed the message.

"Hi, Lydia. It's Gavin. We need to talk." What could we possibly have to talk about after two years of communication blackout? "I know this is out of the blue—" No, I totally expected this. "But can we get together this week?" Gee, my week was pretty full... "Call me, I can make time whenever you're available." Well that's different. He never had time for me when we were engaged.

As I recalled, he only had time for a certain redheaded secretary named Rhonda who wore high heels and short skirts —not that I noticed, but a girl is bound to retain a few details about the woman she finds her significant other of six years balling on his desk when she shows up to surprise him with Chinese food.

Delete or save? Delete or save? Hmmm... I jabbed the delete button with an exuberance usually reserved for a candy spree.

Second message, Saturday, 8:19 a.m.: "Lydia, this is Janice." Jawbreaker called on a Saturday morning? "I'm calling to let you know I e-mailed you directions to the Summer Sail Away. Remember, it's a weekend retreat so pack your jammies and your bikini. And make sure that new hunk of yours packs his too, unless he sleeps in the buff and skinny dips." Yesterday's farce—blissfully forgotten in vodka-rendered memory loss— came crashing back into my aching brain. "Oh, one more thing." I could hear Jawbreaker's smirk. The hair rose on the back of my neck. "Do you have Gavin's email address? I need to zap him the directions, as well. He can't make it Friday, so he's meeting Kelly there on Saturday. Ta ta, see you Monday."

I sat there, blinking like a hummingbird on Pixy Stix. I finally found the capacity to press delete before letting the phone fall to the floor.

If my brain worked, I would probably have tried to figure out how my life had swirled around the bowl so quickly. I reached for the bag of candy in my nightstand drawer before dragging myself, clothed in my candy hearts-covered pajamas, into my workroom. Closing the door behind me, secure in the knowledge that there was no phone, no internet, and no outside distraction in this room, I crossed to the workbench and climbed onto the stool.

I chewed passively on some Swedish Fish.

The workroom was my sanctuary, where I left the outside world and turned inward. It was my stress relief. Some people tried yoga, others skydiving. I made jewelry. It had started when I took jewelry-making as an elective in college, and it just kind of stuck.

What had started as pure hobby became part business when my friend Bethany wanted to stock my designs in her SoHo boutique.

LIV Jewelry was selling like penny candy. For much more than a penny.

Beth couldn't keep it on the shelves. She kept pushing me to hire an assistant, to produce more and take my distribution wider. But that would mean taking my hobby seriously and that might take the fun out the process. For now I just enjoyed working on pieces when the inspiration struck. Like today.

I had a feeling today's sketches would result in some very scary jewelry.

Mentally checking my frustrations at the door, I pulled out a sketch pad and went to work. Dark swirling shapes decorated with spiked starbursts. Heavy lines. Black, midnight blue, and tarnished silver.

The doodles developed into a fine swirl of silver wire with

dark sapphire beads and black onyx stars. I proudly titled the sketch, "Midnight sky."

Setting down my pencil, I pronounced the sketch finished. I glanced up at the clock on the wall to find I had been working for almost two hours.

I produced one sketch and came to one conclusion.

If Gavin was gracing us with his presence at the Summer Sail Away, I was definitely not going singular. Even if it meant a degrading humiliation.

After safely closing all my creativity behind the workroom door, I retrieved my cell. I fidgeted as I waited for her to pick up.

"Yo," she greeted.

This was the moment of no return. I knew I could still back out. And I knew I wouldn't.

"All right, Fi," I said, twirling a candy necklace around my finger, "set me up."

Ready to read the rest? Get *Eye Candy* now.

ABOUT THE AUTHOR

TERA LYNN CHILDS is the RITA-award-winning young adult author of the mythology-based Oh. My. Gods. series, the Forgive My Fins mermaid romance series, the kick-butt monster-hunting Sweet Venom trilogy, and the Darkly Fae series. She also wrote the City Chicks chick lit romance series and co-wrote the Hero Agenda and Creative HeArts series. Tera lives nowhere in particular and spends her time writing wherever she can find a comfy chair and a steady stream of caffeinated beverages. Find her online at *teralynnchilds.com*.

MORE BY TLC

the City Chicks series

Eye Candy

Straight Stalk

Trying Texas

City Chicks (Volume 1)

the Creative HeArts series

Ten Things Sloane Hates About Tru

Falling for the Girl Next Door

the Darkly Fae series

When Magic Sleeps

When Magic Dares

When Magic Burns

When Magic Falls

When Magic Wakes

the Oh. My. Gods. series

Oh. My. Gods.

Goddess Boot Camp

Goddess in Time

the Forgive My Fins series

Forgive My Fins

Fins Are Forever

Just For Fins

Pretty in Pearls

the Sweet Venom trilogy

Sweet Venom

Sweet Shadows

Sweet Legacy

the Hero Agenda series

w/ Tracy Deebs

Powerless

Relentless